CW01064733

YOUNG WRITERS

Word Up!

YOUNG WRITERS' CREATIVE WRITING COMPETITION 2002 FOR SECONDARY SCHOOLS

SOUTH EAST ENGLAND

Edited by Allison Dowse

First published in Great Britain in 2003 by
YOUNG WRITERS
Remus House,
Coltsfoot Drive,
Peterborough, PE2 9JX
Telephone (01733) 890066

HB ISBN 0 75434 144 5
SB ISBN 0 75434 145 3

FOREWORD

This year, Young Writers proudly presents a showcase of the best short stories and creative writing from today's up-and-coming writers.

We set the challenge of writing for one of our four themes - 'Myths & Legends', 'Hold The Front Page', 'A Day In The Life Of . . .' and 'Short Stories/Fiction'. The effort and imagination expressed by each individual writer was more than impressive and made selecting entries an enjoyable, yet demanding, task.

Word Up! South East England is a collection that we feel you are sure to enjoy - featuring the very best young authors of the future. Their hard work and enthusiasm clearly shines within these pages, highlighting the achievement each piece represents.

We hope you are as pleased with the final selection as we are and that you will continue to enjoy this special collection for many years to come.

CONTENTS

The School Of St Helen & St Katharine, Oxfordshire

Catriona Shearer	192
Charlotte Wallace	194
Elizabeth Sharp	196
Hannah Forsyth	199
Daniella Welch	200
Hannah Wilson	201
Fiona Rushbrook	204
Rebecca Green	206
Rebecca Stewart	209
Suzanne Russell	210
Emma Williams	212

Wallington High School For Girls, Surrey

Baleni Balachandran	213
Jane Wilkin	214
Katie Timothy	215
Judith Tang	216
Gabriela Raison	217
Emily King	218
Gabrielle Cooper	219
Meryljo Ching	220
Jessica Trimnell	221
Jennifer Casey	222
Cara Winter	224
Adedoyin Sokan	226
Indusha Selvanathar	227
Stacey Palmer	228
Katherine Moore	229
Catherine Hollis	230
Maria Bryan	231
Rachel Brewer	232
Kimberley Barrow	233
Bernice Tuckey	234
Jessica Bembridge	236

Walthamstow School For Girls, London

The Stories

A DAY IN THE LIFE OF COCO

Usually I leave my clown Coco at home when I go to school. I have always wondered what he gets up to when I'm not there, but I finally managed to find out what he does all day and this is how it begins.

Coco woke up with his friends. It was a cold winter's day and it had snowed overnight. He got dressed and went down for breakfast. After breakfast, he went outside to play with his friends in the snow. He wrapped up warm and he and his friends decided to make a snow clown. It took a long time, but it was worth it, it looked brilliant.

Coco had a lovely lunch. After lunch, he went to play outside. He and his fellow clown friends had a snowball fight, and then they rolled in the snow and made snow angels, then they had tea and for tea they had jacket potatoes with cheese on top. Yummy!

Then I came home from school, Mum and Dad lit the fire, we had some toast and then we played board games, then it was time for bed. I had a hot water bottle and Coco cuddled by the hot water bottle and that is a day in the life of Coco.

Hannah Fitzpatrick (11)

UNFORGETTABLE

I must have only been about nine at the time, my fragile existence had already been through such invisible pain. So it was obvious that I understood him more than anyone else.

To look at him was like looking at a fairy tale, but he was really just like me, he was trapped and it was probably the only way he knew how to escape from it all. He had hair that most Hollywood actors would envy and desire. Although jet-black, to look at it you would swear blind he had the sun trapped inside, the shine would blind your sight of beauty. His lips just begged to be touched by the skin of an angel. Busting with the glow of 1000 red roses blooming in colour.

He used to say that he didn't even have to breathe to make a girl wither, like a flower before him. But like a gentleman, he always knelt down to help them up. His hands were slender and pale but bore a pride that could mould any soul back to life.

But it was his eyes that were the buried treasure of his essence. For they were an enigma to the world, but to those who opened the chest, they were laden with the unforgettable memories that were worth their weight in gold. I saw what lay inside and I have never forgot it because all that was there, I already knew.

So, when he burst through the door, I knew what was going to happen. He ran up to us, spilling out his angelic voice. We all froze, few screamed, but I was all alone and I wasn't scared because I knew that this was all he had left to give. He turned to me and then he ran at me, his face glowed red in the darkness. His outstretched hands grabbed my arms and he swung me over to the side. But, in those brief few moments in which I was airborne, I made eye contact and he flooded me with emotion. As soon as I landed, I knew what he was going to do, but before I could stop him . . .

Bang!

The piercing sound shot through my ears and down she fell, the ice frozen air was broken by the thud of the woman crashing to the floor. I ran to her but she was already dead. Too frail to run away, she never had a chance. I lifted my innocent fingers to her face, I stroked her cheek then I closed her eyes. Everyone was just looking at me, so I got up and slowly walked over to the pathetic figure curled up in the corner. He looked up at me and I looked deeply into his eyes.

'I forgive you,' I told him softly but loud enough for everyone to hear. He stood up in front of me and replied, 'That's all I needed to know. Thank you.' He smiled at me, reached into his pocket and pulled it out, he raised it into the air and then . . .

Bang!

As he fell to the floor, the gun fell from his limp fingers down to the ground below him and the blood drenched the space between us. I knelt down before him, I kissed my fingers and reached out to close his eyes, I then touched his lips and said, 'I'll never forget you, daddy.'

Emma Duggan (15)

MURDER UNJUST

The air was crisp and cold, in the February of 1546 and a mist crept between the gravestones in the ancient churchyard. Every window of the church was shuttered. The moon was blanketed in cloud and giving no guidance through the darkness. In the church, only the dismal echoes of the rain beating on the crumbling roof, broke the silence.

Suddenly, the church doors crashed open and the clouds moved on, filling the church with deformed shadows. In the doorway, silhouetted against the moon, stood a figure in a cloak that blew in the wind. Moving into the damp church, the mysterious figure forced the doors shut. Removing the drenched cloak revealed a handsome young man with hair darker than the night and eyes burning with passion. He searched the darkness for a place to conceal himself. Finally, he saw the entrance to the crypt, his thoughts drifted back to Anne, with her raven hair and angelic smile. A wave of fear swept over him. 'I hope she escaped in time, to London, there she'll be free from that loveless marriage!' he whispered.

The voices were louder now. 'Gabriel Rutkinson, we have her! Your crime is punishable by death, now you both die!' A woman's screams pierced the night air. With a cry of anguish and all hope crushed, Gabriel flung open the church doors. Pistols fired and thick smoke engulfed the murderous scene.

Samantha Butler (15)

A DAY IN THE LIFE OF AN EYEBROW

I'm thick and bushy, I'm on someone's head. This morning I was minding my own business when the person I live on opened a draw and pulled out some tweezers. She plucked some of my eyebrow hairs like I was a chicken and it was so painful. She does it every few months.

Then my owner washed her face and I got really wet. It seemed like we were going to a party because then she put make-up all over her face and eyebrow liner on me. The eye below me kept laughing because the make-up brush tickled him. She spent ages staring in the mirror, then we went to a car. Because I could not see, as my owner has a large fringe, I couldn't tell what was going on, but from my awkward position, I could tell we were going to a party, as there were four other girls with us in the car.

We got out and went into a large house - *nooooo* - it was a sleepover! These are the worst places for eyebrows to be. The eyes below were moaning when they discovered the dreadful news.

I decided to have a little doze for a while, then I woke up to find . . . everyone was sitting in a circle with a bottle in the middle. One girl spun it and it landed on my owner, then the girl said something. I looked down and my owner didn't look very happy, then the ears, (who heard what the girl who spun the bottle had said, whispered to me.) Oh no! I was filled with dread. According to the ears this was a dare game and my owner had been dared to . . . I can't say it!

Anyway, one of the girls handed her a shaver and my owner brought it towards me, the other girls were laughing. I was sweating so much, all the make-up and liner I was wearing came off. I was filled with dread as slowly, my owner shaved the other eyebrow, then came over to me. This wasn't a dare, this was murder, I thought as I looked where the other eyebrow had lived for years.

Owww! Ouch! That was it, I had been shaved. Give me a few weeks though, I'll be back!

Emma Ryle (13)
Babington House School, Kent

A DAY IN THE LIFE OF A CHIMNEY

Hello, my name is Charlotte Chimney Owenite (street). All chimneys are named after the name of our street. For example, my next-door neighbour is Bostall Lane and I have some friends in Congress Road and some in Greening Street. When we are built, the builders give you a name and put chimney in the middle, the name of your street and, voila - you have a name.

Being a chimney is very lonely during the day because you can't talk to your friends because you are breaking the chimney code. The nights are really groovy, all the chimneys getting their chimney grooves on. On the second of every month each street has to get together and organise a disco. But snooty chimneys on the lane of Marmaduke are very snooty but we don't let that ruin our fun.

In the summer we are all healthy, whereas in the winter I have always got a tickly cough. That is because they have always got a fire on. They have no consideration at all. It's not that lonely, some days, in the winter I get a little boy visitor, that day my cough is fine.

Not all chimneys like their family that live in them. Some people don't even use their chimneys and some don't treat their chimneys very nicely. Whereas, my family are really nice to me. I get cleaned out twice a week in the winter and twice a month in the summer. That is quite generous. My mate Charlene Chimney Clifton (Avenue), well, her family only clean her out once a month in the winter. She is always coughing. Oh, and they never clean her out in the summer.

Do you know what I heard? The Queen cleans all of her chimneys every night. They must be the healthiest chimneys ever. I bet they know about every war, every argument, every idea, they are *soooo* lucky.

Oh, you heard me talk about the chimney code, well, the rules are:

1. Never talk during the day.
2. Always spread the gossip.
3. If someone sees you or hears you, let everyone know so they can be careful.
4. Be nice to your fellow chimneys on the chimney code.

They are the main ones, if I said them all, we'd be here for a month. Well, I hope this gives you an idea on how chimneys like to be treated. Goodbye!

(The moral of this story is be nice to your chimney.)

Anna Philpott (13)
Babington House School, Kent

A DAY IN THE LIFE OF A PUDDLE

Here we go again. The water cycle is about to start. My brothers and sisters wait until the moment is right and then, like a shower of glitter falling down to Earth, our cloud bursts and fall to a different country every time.

This time, I saw grass with people and their umbrellas running to get out of the rain. I don't know why they do it. I think that my family are quite delightful.

I landed on some hard stuff, which I think people call concrete and one by one, saw a few members of my family drop into the same puddle. I'm glad I'm not alone, as I know that the sun will probably dry us up. Last time we were on top of a mountain and got caught up in a glacier so we ended up in a river. That's why we're in the water cycle again.

Once the cloud closed and disappeared my brothers and sisters were still as we wanted to see where we were. To my horror, I saw that we were in a park.

Then, just what we all were thinking, children with their wellies came along, as well as a dog. The children jumped in our puddle and my brother Spark was parted from us, in another puddle where birds were coming down to have a drink of water. Oh, this was terrible. Where's Sparkle, Spark's twin sister? What about Dew? I'm losing everyone. All that's left are Glitter, Drop, Pale and I.

We're in such an open space, anything could happen. While we were reflecting we saw some birds fly over us and even Pale went paler in the freezing temperature in our puddle.

After a while, when we were all comforting each other, the sun came out and it was havoc once again.

This man with a foot the size of our puddle, stepped into us and Drop was soaked up in his sock, Pale was splashed a little way off and immediately got dried up. Glitter and I were together when we were dried up. We said that this was going to be a new life in Puddle Lane.

Sarah Berry (13)
Babington House School, Kent

A Day In The Life Of A Shell

I have travelled long distances, crossed many seas, I have been to many countries and have laid on many shores, admiring the hot temperatures.

My body is a pearly white colour with hints of gold; I am coloured all over with tiny ripples. If you pick me up and put me to your ear you can hear the many oceans I have sailed.

Can you guess what I am? Yes, that's right, I am a shell and today I'm going to take you on one of the many adventures in my life.

It's now 9am, I can tell because the sun has just settled in the sky, and the sea tide is coming in. As the wind blows the silky sand across my body, the waves flow towards me. As I watch, silently at the sea, I see sailing boats with high sails and fancy names filled with people float past me.

It has now gone past 1 o'clock and the tide is getting rougher. The tourists that were lying in the hot sun, have packed up their belongings and have gone home, taking some of my friends with them.

The sea comes closer, sweeping me into the ocean, once again my journey will continue, but who knows where I will end up this time?

Georgina Alder (13)
Babington House School, Kent

A DAY IN THE LIFE OF A MIRROR

I am cleaned every day with a cloth and Mr Sheen's window spray. The maid comes every day and rubs the dust off my shiny skin. I'm looked at every time someone walks down the stairs and before they walk out of the door. When they are looking pretty, they praise me, when they look bad, they put me down.

They squeeze their spots in front of me, spraying the water that comes out of them. They put their make-up on in front of me, waving their powder on my clean face.

When they go on holiday or when they go out, I am left alone staring at the wall. It is quiet and peaceful, but when they get back, it is noisy until they go to sleep. If they are gossiping, I am the first to hear or if they are fighting, I get front row seats.

Faye James (13)
Babington House School, Kent

A DAY IN THE LIFE OF AN ELECTRIC GUITAR OWNED BY MARK HOPPUS!

Being Mark Hoppus' guitar is quite an honour! He is part of a brilliant punk rock band called Blink 182. *They rock!*

Mark has many guitars, hanging in plastic cases around his house, but I am definitely his favourite.

Whenever he practises, he uses me. Whenever he goes on tour, he uses me, except at the end of the show when he sometimes smashes one of his not so nice guitars, into a thousand pieces! *Not fun!*

Mark has played some excellent songs on me. Songs such as 'The Rock Show', 'What's My Age Again' and 'Stay Together For The Kids', (my favourite!) I'm sure that there will be many more songs to come, because Mark is such a good writer!

I love being Mark's guitar. The tours, the practises and everything else there is. The screaming fans, you can feel the heat and atmosphere they create! Once again I am proud to say that I am Mark Hoppus' bass guitar!

Katy Fieldhouse (13)
Babington House School, Kent

THE CHANGING ROOM MIRROR

Day in, day out, people looking ugly, smart, scruffy, weird, casual, grungy, sporty and formal, and believe me, there are lots more. They come into the shop, see me, stop, run their fingers through their hair, do a pose and maybe squeeze the odd spot or pick the blackhead from their noses! You get so many people who think they look nice but they look terrible and sometimes it scares me and I close my eyes! I dread little kids and sometimes I open my door so that they fall down as punishment for putting their sticky fingers on me!

My beautiful, golden, gleaming frame makes me glisten when the sun comes in!

I have a best friend who comes to see me every Monday, Wednesday and Friday. She smothers me with clean kisses and her perfume she sprays, clings to me, Mr Sheen it's called, I think! Her yellow handkerchief swipes my body and glides round my frame, like a ballerina on ice.

Lauren Obertelli-Leahy (13)
Babington House School, Kent

THE DAY IN THE LIFE OF A SPOT!

Oh, it's a hard life being a spot, trying to live as long as possible in somewhere always very unpleasant.

The mornings are the worst, being woken up at some ungodly hour by the human I am occupying, staggering off to the mirror to check what's becoming of me.

I end up seeing an ugly and extremely unfriendly human staring straight back at me. I am surprised she doesn't crack the mirror.

Then, comes the sharp fingernails, poking at me until I feel almost ready to explode from all my insides.

Then, as I am ready to explode, out comes the Clearasil, burning me and absorbing me into a tissue and I feel myself evaporating to spot heaven!

Don't forget humans. *I'll be back!*

Lauren Patterson (12)
Babington House School, Kent

A DAY IN THE LIFE OF A BEACH

The wind flutters like a butterfly and touches your skin like a mother's love. It whistles through your ears and echoes like a harmonic choir drifting into the daydreams of the morning.

If you stand, just stand and relax, all you can hear is the pitter-patter of the crab's legs running on the rocks and the sound of fish gliding their fins through the fresh water.

Along the beach the shells lay cemented onto the sand beds soaking up the sun. The shells capture the sounds of the rippling sea and the crunching of the sand. The tide creeps in like a leopard waiting to catch its prey, engulfing the sand and rocks, destroying its path like a tornado, but still it looks calm and peaceful. A human eye would not see or feel its enormous power.

Gradually life emerges. In the heat of the day, the sun is captured in the grove like a greenhouse. Everyone feels lethargic. The sand is heated like lava, and the sea warms like a hot spring. The tide is in. At first it is like a warm pond, but soon it turns into a playground.

As the heat gradually lifts from the hot day the water is evaporated from in between the particles of the sand. The sand is left damp and moist. It is no longer dry and dusty.

The beach is now deserted with no habitation; just the sand and the sea have each other for company. The sun sets over the horizon and the power of the sun fades. The day in the life of this beach has come to an end.

Bonnie Jackson (13)
Babington House School, Kent

LEGEND OF THE SEA STALLION

This is a legend that took place off the coast of Cornwall, several years ago. Fishermen still tell it today, but no one knows the truth.

Off the coast of Cornwall in 1990, in the village of Mousehole, there was a small fisherman's hut, where the man who saw the legend, lived.

The day was cold and wet and many people returned to their cosy cottages in the village. When night fell, all that could be seen were little balls of light in the windows of the cottages, and there was a gentle sound of creaking fishing boats, rocking slowly in the Mousehole gap.

At the stroke of twelve, it came. As the fisherman emerged from his hut, a gentle wind blew through the harbour. As the old man stood on the wall staring at the sea, whistling with the wind, there was a sudden clap of thunder and the sea turned rough. Without warning, a screeching neigh sounded through the wind and storm. Suddenly, a huge, grey stallion came crashing through the waves. As the stallion reared up through the building waves, water flew up and over the harbour wall.

Soon the storm died down and the fisherman silently looked up, to see the stallion standing right in front of him, on the other side of the wall, silent now. Very slowly, the fisherman reached out to touch the nose of the stallion, but it faded away into the fog.

The fisherman never lived to tell the tale of his meeting with the stallion, but it was seen again, two years later by another fisherman, who had the same experience. No one knows when it will make its appearance again.

Louise Pritchard (12)
Blenheim High School, Surrey

WHY?

I just stood there. Just stood there and watched it happen. How . . . how could I just watch? You don't know how much it hurts to see a loved one die. And deep down, knowing that it's your fault. I felt like something had ripped a part of my soul out and nothing will fill the empty hole your death has given me. I'm sorry everyone. I'm so sorry. I let my power get the better of me, and I was blinded by it. He said . . . he said he was proud of me. But how can he be proud of me when I let him die? Mum says she doesn't blame me, and that I shouldn't blame myself. If only I'd listened to him and finished sooner. I wish it was me instead. I wish I could take his place.

Dad, you loved life so much, that you sacrificed yourself to save it. I let you down Dad; I let everybody down. You alone saw my power for what it was and you put so much faith in me. I failed you. I know you are watching Mum and me, and I wish you were here with us now. After everything we've been through, I wanted it to be like old times. When we'd go fishing and Mum would wait and shout at us when we got back. I will uphold your honour, Dad. I will fight for your memory.

Nicola Clark (14)
Coloma Convent Girls' School, Surrey

A SHORT STORY

'Sshh Lottie, he'll hear us!'
'Maisie, this undertaker building is massive, how will he hear us?'
'He is a mastermind criminal and thief, I wouldn't be surprised if he set up a device of ears all over the place! Anything to help him get his hands on the Heart of Gold!'
Beep! Beep!
'Here we are, Dr Millicent says the heart's in room 141! He doesn't know where the thief is though!'
'That's great! We've got to make our way to room 141, and there's a criminal about and we don't know where he is! Do you realise how dangerous this is?'
'Come on, let's move, before he hears you whining!'

'How many of these revolting corridors do we have to -?'
'Here we are, room 141 . . .'
'About time! Maisie, what are you doing?'
'Checking the room's empty with this supersonic scanner Dr Millicent gave me. We don't want to rush in on a mastermind criminal now do we? It's empty. Quick, before he comes back!'
'God, that light's strong enough to blind someone!'
'It's the Heart of Gold!'
'Maisie, the light!'
'Oh, I forgot, put on these glasses to protect your eyes, Dr Millicent gave them to me!'

Back at the laboratory

'There seems to be a bit of a problem . . .'
'Doctor, what's wrong?'
'The light of the heart is fading. The real Heart of Gold shines constantly . . . strange.'
'Look Doctor!'
'Why, it's burning into ashes! Wait, there's a note,

'The *Heart of Gold's* not hard to find,
It is inside the one that's kind.
Just because the body has stopped,
It doesn't mean the heart can be swapped.
The heart was born with her in Heaven
And back there they will go together'.

Sally Gannon (14)
Coloma Convent Girls' School, Surrey

NO WAY OUT

A few days ago, something extraordinary and unusual happened at one of the UK's top theme parks: Thorpe Park. Thorpe Park has been known for its scary and horrendous rides, but this extravagant story, which I'm about to explain to you, will have you on tenterhooks.

Several people entered the 'No Way Out' ride and by reading this name you will soon be able to find out what mysterious things have happened at this adventurous place. Many people were screaming their heads off during this uncomfortable roller coaster ride, when suddenly the bumpy and rough ride stopped, out of the blue. As well as the ride being brought to a halt, the people who were enjoying themselves on the journey of a lifetime, disappeared unexpectedly. This wasn't part of the roller coaster's daily routine, and even experts were horrified by this event.

A man who worked there said, 'I couldn't believe my eyes when I was watching the ride from my little room. One minute, the people were enjoying themselves silly, and the next they vanished without a trace. The noise abruptly became as quiet as a mouse.'

Till this day the people and the 'No Way Out' ride have still not been found. This tragic story is like what people say about the Bermuda Triangle. Experts suspect that a magician of some kind did this, so that they could blackmail the Thorpe Park director to get money in exchange for the ride and the individuals. What do you think?

Sinitta Fernandes (14)
Coloma Convent Girls' School, Surrey

MYTHS AND LEGENDS

In Cornwall it is reported that a black cat-like animal prowls the fields looking for food. The animal is bigger than a lion but smaller than a horse.

It has reportedly attacked many farmers' livestock and small children who have been playing in the fields. Many local people are losing business and are scared that the animal might attack another child. There are many pictures of this animal and at first everyone thought it was a panther, but it is too big, so nobody knows exactly what the animal is. The animal will keep coming back because it knows there is food there. The locals have also seen the animal on the streets and many people live in fear of going outside just in case it attacks.

One eyewitness said that the cat-like animal had bright blue eyes which you could see from a mile off. He said he was walking home one night and he could see these bright blue eyes floating in the air, but as he got closer he could see the animal's teeth and other features.

Many farmers have set up a neighbourhood watch and they are armed with guns, so if they see the animal they will either shoot or try to scare it off. This animal has affected many people's lives but when people go looking for it they never find it. The animal has been reported to be in this area for hundreds of years.

Katie Law (14)
Coloma Convent Girls' School, Surrey

THE GIFT

I stared at the padded brown envelope that stared back at me; with its stamp-marked eyes. I suppose I had been expecting it really. After everything else that had happened, it was bound to come sooner or later.

It all started about five months ago, a couple of days after my brother was born. You see, I had fallen in with a bad crowd. By that I mean a group of seventeen-year-olds, doing drugs, muggings, and everything else associated with those things. Anyway, I decided one day that this was not the lifestyle I was going to lead, so I broke off from the gang. It all started because they thought I would go to the police or something. I told them it wasn't like that! I just wanted a change.

My pleas did not stop the phone calls, the threats and the visits. It did not stop the writing scribbled on the wall at the front of our council flat - *It's not a good idea* - I was scared, really terrified of those who had been my closest peers.

So, when the post arrived this morning and a parcel addressed to *Dearest Susie Baldrik*, arrived with it, I knew it must be from *them*. The name, that's how they knew. How someone can get Susie from Rebecca is anyone's guess. But that's what *they* called me, Susie.

I picked up the parcel in both hands, hesitating momentarily, deciding whether it would be best to just leave the package unopened. No. Out of sight, but not out of mind. I prised my forefinger under the sticky strip and tore away at the top of the envelope. I poured the contents of the package out onto the crumbling sideboard and looked. They had done well this time, boy, it was a good one. Good enough to have me sweating and shaking at the sight I saw before me. From what I did see, the small bundled mass, I knew this was just the beginning.

Hannah Macadam (14)
Coloma Convent Girls' School, Surrey

A DAY IN THE LIFE OF A CHILD
FROM WORLD WAR II

Life is hell! I don't know who to turn to, it's just noise, noise, noise! Mum's in hospital and has been all night. Dad's been beating her up you see. She was trying to convince him not to go to war but he was drunk, as always, and hit her too hard. Dad didn't let me see her, he just locked me in the shed. This morning he opened it up and let me out but I couldn't find Mum anywhere at home. It was then that Dad told me she was in hospital and he made up some ridiculous story that she'd drank too much gin and had fallen and hit her head. I can't believe that he actually thought I'd believe it. I'm not a kid!

Anyway, at the moment, I'm in a bomb shelter. The bomb siren went off about an hour ago and we're still not allowed to leave. Why can't they understand, I just want to see my mum. I'm meant to be in the countryside but Mum didn't want me to go. She says that if we're all going to die, then we might as well all die together. Dad didn't like her saying that and he gave her a clip round the ear for it.

At the moment I've got a really bad tummy ache. The pain is excruciating and I think it's my diarrhoea coming back again. I'm still wearing the same clothes that I wore then. I can smell myself, it's vile!

Diana Main (14)
Coloma Convent Girls' School, Surrey

A DAY IN THE LIFE OF A CUB

The glistening sun peeps over the hills as Mother goes searching for food. My two brothers and me are too young to go with her. 'Maybe in a few weeks,' she tells us, 'it's a cruel world out there.' But what's so bad? Apparently there are nasty people who dislike us and will treat us badly. We are just friendly animals that want to play!

I'm bored and need an adventure. I tell my hungry brothers that I am going to look for Mother while I go to find out what the world's really about. I sneak through the prickly bushes and listen out for human voices - I think it's all clear! The trees are getting less as I creep through the park. The sun still hasn't fully risen - there shouldn't be many people around. The creak of an old iron gate catches my attention as I walk out onto the road.

I'm scared - the cold, sharp wind is whistling by me. There's light coming towards me. I have frozen. What is it? A big monster roaring with two gleaming eyes. I try to run but my feet won't move - it's getting closer! *Phew,* I just made it! I managed to run onto the pavement before it reached me. I take a final glimpse of this *thing*. Silly me it's just a car. *Never again will I ignore Mother.* It looks like I am too small to face the world on my own after all.

Danielle Padfield (14)
Coloma Convent Girls' School, Surrey

STRANGE HAPPENINGS IN A SMALL ALLEY

She walked down the alley, glancing over her shoulder repeatedly, as if she was being followed. She was tall, in a dark business suit, with a large briefcase in one hand. Her hand gripped the briefcase, her knuckles white with strain. Her hair was cut short, in a bob and she brushed a strand, which had strayed out of place, from her face. Her green eyes were the only pinpricks of light in the alley.

She stopped abruptly as a dark figure loomed out of the darkness.
'You've got the stuff?' a male voice sounded loud and harsh.
'Keep your voice down Harry, do you want us to get discovered?'
Harry scratched his head, 'I'll do what I want,' he growled. 'Marie, where's the stuff?'
'I don't know and I won't know until you keep your voice down,' she hissed.
'Alright,' he snarled, 'but I'm warning you, one false move and,' he drew his hand across his throat and made a bloodcurdling noise.
'Alright, alright,' amended Marie hurriedly. Harry was pleased to notice she was panicking. 'I won't make any mistakes.'
'Good,' he snarled.
'Right,' she gulped nervously, 'here.' She pushed the briefcase into his hands. 'That's all of it. Harry I don't want anything more to do with this. Alright?' She turned to go. 'If you do anything to try to meet me again, I'll call the cops!' When she turned round completely, he whipped out a pistol and shot three times at her figure. 'You won't be doing anything missy,' he snarled and then he threw his head back and laughed. She fell to the ground with a thud, her head rolling to one side. A bird circled above them, calling, calling . . .

Alicia Williams (14)
Coloma Convent Girls' School, Surrey

A DAY IN THE LIFE OF BRITNEY SPEARS

5:55am

I've just been awoken by my Justin Timberlake clock. I am drained already. Imagine retiring to bed at 1am and waking up five hours later!

I have to go to the studio to practise for tonight's concert, the best in town this year: *Let's hit the road, LA!* Anyway, had better get dressed.

6:15am

I'm just getting into my Lamborghini and heading for the *Saucy Studio*.

6.35am

'You're late!' is the greeting I get from my manager. Anyhow, we will now go over all the songs I'm singing tonight.

12:15pm

We've just finished rehearsals and boy am I tired! We're having lunch now. We'll have to practice a few bits again, then go home and get ready to party!

5:30pm

I'm on my way home. I have to be back on stage in two and a half hours. I'm tired already! My whole family is coming - my mum, Jamie Lynn, Justin and some of my cousins. This is going to be a great night!

7:40pm

I'm now backstage and the amount of people is spectacular! I'm a bit nervous but happy that I have millions of fans supporting me.

7:59pm

I'm just about to go on and sing *Baby One More Time!*

8:15pm

This is amazing! Everyone's enjoying this! I have to change my clothes for *Slave 4 U* and then, back on stage again.

9:30pm
We're halfway through and Justin is doing a speech - oh no - he wants me to go back on!

12am
It's finished and everyone's exhausted! I can't wait to get home!

1am
I'm going to bed,
            goodnight!

Lisa Dias (13)
Coloma Convent Girls' School, Surrey

A DAY IN THE LIFE OF A BLACK SLAVE IN 1775

It's my third day on the plantations, the master has changed my name and I have no family. The master has warned us not to do anything we're not supposed to or he'll chop a part of our body off or put a mask on us just to show the others what will happen to them if they do it.

Today is harvest, I have to cut down the sugar cane and then take it to the mill. 'Hi Arbo, are you going to come to the fields, we can't be late now,' I said.
'Yes okay, I'll be right with you,' he replied.

It's a hard day, all we do is cut the sugar cane and then take it to the mill all day. The girls sing to pass time, one girl sings a line and everyone else repeats it. The overseer lets us do this, the overseer is mean when he has his whip, he will strike you for almost anything.

Our master, Will, lets us go into the woods at night and have celebrations of religion and we sing and dance all night long, but in the morning we have to go to his church and then work again. It's a tiring day and at night I go back to my mud and straw hut, make some food and then got to sleep. I do not mind being a slave but I would much rather not be one, but I can live with it.

Charlie Severn (13)
Coloma Convent Girls' School, Surrey

A DAY IN THE LIFE OF MARTIN LUTHER KING

It was a cold winter's day in Washington and I had just sat down to a hot cup of cocoa, when the doorbell rang. It was Jennifer at the door, she was a charity aid worker. I gave her my last dime and sat back down to my cup of cocoa and read the morning newspaper.

I couldn't believe my eyes, I was reading about another racist attack in the south. Black people and white people are set different rules against each other and we even have different toilets to go to, because of the colour of our skin.

It was seven o'clock in the morning now and I had to go to work. I finished getting dressed and put on my hat and scarf because it started to snow. I was waiting at the bus stop waiting for my usual bus, when some white men came along and I suffered a lot of racial abuse. They called me all sorts of names like; 'Your skin is coal and you are a black nigger.' This hurt me a lot because there were about ten of them and one of me.

I stepped onto the bus and was forced to stand up because white people got to sit down. I thought that this wasn't right and it was time something changed!

Lauren Girvan (13)
Coloma Convent Girls' School, Surrey

A DAY IN THE LIFE OF A POOR, HOMELESS PERSON

25th December 1999
Yet another lonely Christmas. No friends, no money, no family - nothing. I hate this time of year. Everyone is so happy with family and friends. I'd give anything to be with someone I love. I want to gather around the beautifully decorated table, eat the delicious food and sit under the Christmas tree opening presents. Why is it always so sad for me at this time of year?

31st December 1999
People are now gathering on the streets of London. I have received a few pennies from some generous people. People are dressed up and out with loved ones to have a good time. People are looking merry, while I am looking sad. I am hurting inside. I am going to celebrate the new millennium alone. I want someone to pick me off the street and take me away to a good place.

A little boy comes running in my direction. He stops a few paces from me. The boy quite reminded me of when I was younger, a scruffy little boy with big brown eyes. He had something behind his back. I told the boy to go away. He stood there then he came a little closer to me. He then took out the object from behind his back. The boy offered me a sandwich and a little orange toy car. The little boy made my day. I was so happy. I tried to thank him but the boy ran off into the busy crowds.

Suddenly the clock struck twelve. '3, 2, 1, Happy New Year!' What a new year!

Amaka Uche (13)
Coloma Convent Girls' School, Surrey

THE MISTAKE

It was a tropical day and I was feeling neglected. We were in the centre of Spain and my beloved mum and boring dad had gone off for a cocktail and a sunbathe by the poolside.

My mum and I had an argument this morning, because she forgot to pack my pink checked bikini. I shouted at her, she and Dad just walked out. That was my favourite bikini and I had wanted to bring it just for my holiday. It was time for my mum's punishment.

I sat on a sinking green sofa wondering what I could do. Then, on the side was my mum's tablets to encourage hair growth. So I carried them down to the poolside where she was. They both had their lazy eyes closed and looked very peaceful. I threw five of the yellow tablets in her drink and watched them fizz to the bottom. I ran back to our apartment giggling.

Suddenly I heard my mum crying and screaming, so I jumped up and looked out of the window. My mum and dad were running. They burst open the door and my dad (taking off the towel from my mother's head) said, 'Look what's happened to mother.'
I looked. My mum had grown facial hair, a beard and a moustache. 'How can this have happened?' cried Mum. 'I never take more than the recommended dose of those tablets.'
'You never know what they put in cocktails these days, Mum,' I replied guiltily.

Katy Brown (14)
Coloma Convent Girls' School, Surrey

THE MISTAKE

It was a hardworking day for an old man as he was taming wild animals. At the time he was building and repairing cages for the animals. At seven o'clock the missus came out because she said that she felt neglected, so she helped him mend the cages.

Soon after Josie went in, because Tom, her husband, wanted to do something illegal: (without her knowing) set a trap for the wolves and then kill them. He set out very doubtfully and there was complete silence, apart from the howling wolves. He knew he was in a lot of danger because the wolves were very vicious, they were hunting for food day and night. It took him around about half an hour to fix the trap and when he did, he ran as fast as he could back to the house.

Josie wanted to have a conversation with Tom about labour, she said she wanted to start earning money and start working, so they could extend their house and garden.
Tom just said, 'Yes, whatever you want darling.'
She said, 'Well, I will start tomorrow.'

In the morning Tom got up really early to go to the woods to check if there were any wolves trapped. Tom could see some movement by the traps, the leaves were rustling. Tom thought to himself, yes I have got a wolf without getting caught. He went to the trap and saw . . . the ranger. The ranger shouted, 'Get me out of here!'

Lea Galea (14)
Coloma Convent Girls' School, Surrey

A DAY OF FEAR

One fine Saturday morning I got dressed and arranged to meet up with my friends. We strolled around for a while and then went to sit down and watch a bit of television in the store. We slowly scrolled through the channels and we ended up watching the news, only to see the headline: *London centre in danger of a bomb attack.* My friends and I gasped and looked at each other in shock. We were really worried and scared but we took it slowly and didn't rush. We stayed calm for one another.

After that we went to my house and discussed it in my bedroom. As soon as my mother and father came home we broke the news to them. They said, 'Don't worry, the news is just giving people a warning.'
My friends and I turned to each other and began to laugh. We had been so silly we had just jumped to conclusions once again. We learnt our lesson from this, we should make sure of what we listen to and not make a mountain out of a molehill. It was definitely a day of fear for us but now it seems just like a dream.

Gabriella Cappello (14)
Coloma Convent Girls' School, Surrey

THE MISTAKE

You could see my dad was nervous as he gripped his glass of wine. Then the toastmaster shouted for the speech. My dad stood rigid as he began to talk. Thank God the dialogue wasn't tedious.

My sister, Nina, in her beautiful dress, looked so proud as he spoke. But then he made a small mistake, he called my sister, Nina me, Chloe. It was a small mistake but big enough for the people that were drunk to look at me and then laugh at my dad.

After that mistake he kept tripping up on words and stopping mid-sentence. You could hear his so-called friends laughing at him. Among others, you could see the bride getting more embarrassed and upset.

For the rest of the night my dad was silent, not saying a word to anybody. I went up to him and told him to enjoy the night and not to dwell on the past. I told him to go round and talk to people. I saw a few people who were too lazy to go and say sorry or tell him to forget about it.

The night was almost over but my dad was still angry. We said goodbye to everyone as they left. I still think he thinks about it.

Chloé Hawkins (14)
Coloma Convent Girls' School, Surrey

A Day In The Life Of A Butterfly

Sitting on the oak tree was a dark brown shell which was holding inside a miracle. A chance for a part of nature to be transformed into something completely different.

Inside was an obese caterpillar having a long nap whilst waiting for the right time to come. In his head he was hoping he'd be beautiful, convincing himself he'd be beautiful, pleading he'd be beautiful.

Had the time come? The cocoon began to shake. Slowly but surely a little head appeared out of the gap and stared around at the world. Everything was bright and wonderful. It looked completely different when he was a caterpillar.

Next, he hurled himself out of the cocoon and stood proudly on a nearby branch. He fluttered his new wings and opened them fully to reveal all the colours of the rainbow that were on his back. He was beautiful at last.

He decided to fly up high in the air. He cautiously stumbled to the edge of the branch and leapt off. He couldn't believe he could fly. He circled round and round. He landed on a sweet smelling flower and flew off again, higher and higher. He became more dangerous and daring and flew down to a red and white checked blanket. He saw a mysterious glass jar and landed next to it. A towering hand placed the jar over him. He was caught.

Caitriona Joyce (13)
Coloma Convent Girls' School, Surrey

THE GIFT

I opened my eyes, sat up quickly and gasped with excitement. I could hear the birds singing their cheerful tune and could see the sun peeping between the gap in the curtains. I jumped out of bed and stumbled around in the dark, trying to make my way to the light switch and then to my calendar. I looked at it and I could feel a broad smile appear on my face. At last the day that I had been waiting for all year had arrived. I was so overwhelmed with excitement that I lost track of time. I looked at my watch and found that I was going to be late for school.

I was rushing around like a headless chicken, trying to find my uniform. I got dressed in record time and had ten minutes to spare. I made my way down the stairs as fast as I could, then into the living room.

There was a huge pile of presents standing in the middle of the floor. Mum came in, 'Happy birthday love,' she said.

I started unwrapping. After, as I was tidying up, there was a knock on the door. I opened it and the postman handed me a parcel. I sat down on the stairs and opened it. After one layer of paper came another then another, until I got to a small red box. I opened it and there it was staring back at me . . .

Laura Gallagher (14)
Coloma Convent Girls' School, Surrey

LAETITIA COMES CLEAN

The rumours are true, we have it on good authority that Laetitia Kingson is married. Her spokesperson finally gave in to our demands and told us all that everyone had been dying to find out.

For two years now, Laetitia has been going out with PJ Dunkirk. They have been spotted by our cameramen leaving restaurants like *The Ivy* and *The Holly*, holding hands! The only problem is they never stop to say hello before they're whisked away in a black limo. But we have still faithfully brought you pictures of the pair whenever they've been seen.

The wedding took place in a registry office, which is very strange as most celebs these days marry in style, in a big castle in Ireland. Laetitia and PJ say they are above the 'hype' and chose a simple, quiet wedding, with just friends and family, according to their spokespeople.

Laetitia will not be taking PJ's surname as it reminds her too much of World War II and it's so depressing that she doesn't want to be called Mrs Dunkirk.

Laetitia Kingson and PJ Dunkirk are part of the world of the beautiful people, so however much they try, they will end up living in luxury. We say why not, if you can afford it!

We wish both Laetitia and PJ the best of luck and hope they last longer than it takes to eat a bacon sarnie; or longer than J Lo's marriage did.

Lucy Hobson (14)
Coloma Convent Girls' School, Surrey

MYTHS AND LEGENDS - EARDSWOP

About six centuries ago, there lived a colony of curious creatures called Eardswop. Eardswop were very strange creatures, their skin was a pale, mottled green and they had vibrant purple eyes and hair, but the most bizarre thing about them was their purple wings on their feet! Of course, these creatures weren't very big, only about five inches high!

For a while, the Eardswop and humans had lived in harmony. You see, the Eardswop's hair made the most beautiful strings for musical instruments, no other strings would play quite as well. So the Eardswop would have their hair cut by humans and as pay, the humans would keep the hair and make their instruments.

However, one day a human found a dead Eardswop and decided to use his hair. Whilst cutting the Eardswop's hair, the knife slipped and he cut off a piece of wing. He pushed it to one side, thinking he would clear it later.

The next morning, the whole family were found dead. When the townsfolk investigated they found a tiny wing in the cooking pot and realised what had happened.

The townsfolk were scared. They realised that these tiny creatures could poison them all, so they went out and burnt them all and their bodies fell to the ground but their hair grew into the grass and left a reminder of them for centuries to come.

So if you ever see a purple thistle, remember the Eardswop.

Lucy Baker (14)
Coloma Convent Girls' School, Surrey

THE MISTAKE

'I'll be home early tonight, darling.'

'OK Mum,' I replied, although I wasn't really listening. I knew all too well what was going to follow.

'Don't be late for school and don't even think about skipping breakfast.'

'Yes Mum.' I said sarcastically.

'I'm being serious Lauren,' she said, shutting the door behind her. She left for work at about 8am and I left for school about ten minutes later.

School was so boring that day. I wanted some excitement, some wild adventure, but I never expected what followed that afternoon to happen.

I got home at normal time, but the house felt strange as soon as I entered. I was certain something was wrong. As I hung my blazer on a peg, I heard a noise. It wasn't very loud, but definitely a noise. That's when I worked out that there was a burglar in the house. The weird thing was I didn't feel scared.

Several more noises led me through the kitchen to the utility room. I grabbed a rolling pin and raised it above my head. I opened the door. I closed my eyes and swung the rolling pin over the burglar's body. The scream that followed was high-pitched and dread shot through me as I opened my eyes to see my mum lying motionless on the floor.

Clare Conway (14)
Coloma Convent Girls' School, Surrey

THE MISTAKE

The baby was crying. Sarah, my three-year-old, was poking her and I was going to be late. The telly was on and Sarah had turned on the radio. The baby's crying just kept getting louder! I had the toast under the grill because the stupid toaster was acting up again. Ever since my boyfriend had left me I hadn't had enough money to pay the bills, let alone fix anything!

'Waa!' The baby was getting louder.
'Sarah! Leave your sister alone, if you don't want a sore backside!' I looked at my watch. I was already late. Where was the childminder? The phone was ringing and someone was at the door (it was just a package). I had to go. If I was late for work again, I'd be fired!

I kissed the baby, turned off the TV and radio and told Sarah the childminder wouldn't be long, grabbed my bag and left.

That was the biggest mistake of my life!

While I was gone the toast burnt and the grill went up in flames. That phone call was the childminder saying she couldn't come today. The baby was in her highchair in the kitchen but luckily Sarah heard her and rescued her from the kitchen's hot inferno.

I came home and saw the skeleton of my house. My girls were okay. Phew! My girls were okay! I kept saying that. It wasn't so bad.

Nicola Velasco (14)
Coloma Convent Girls' School, Surrey

THE DAILY MALE

He Said What?

Prince Harry has recently revealed that he's not very good at polo and hates the game. He was heard telling a friend, 'I think the sport is awfully boring and so I don't try that hard with it. I only do it because of Dad.'

A spokeswoman for the palace confirmed what was heard and said, 'William and Harry have been taught the sport since they were very young but unfortunately, Harry never cottoned on to it. William took to it like a fish to water, but Harry always had difficulties'.

The 17-year-old prince has been facing a lot of problems recently with the tragic death of his mother five years ago and recent brushes with the law. Now this has come out, his father is devastated. Prince Charles has always been proud of his boys and so was surprised when one of his pride and joy told him they didn't like the royal game. He has treated the boys very well all their lives and he thought teaching polo would be another good thing, as it's what his father taught him as a child, so in a way he wanted to keep up the family tradition.

Prince William was questioned about this and he said he'd always known about his brother's dislike of the sport, but didn't say anything because he knew it would upset their father.

Although this news has come to light, Harry will continue playing in teams and clubs as before.

Natalie Hanlon (14)
Coloma Convent Girls' School, Surrey

HOLD THE FRONT PAGE

Will 4 Britney

Exclusive! Prince William has been seen snogging Britney Spears!

The two were spotted at a top London hotel swapping saliva. Britney is over in London promoting her new song, *Boys*.

It's never been a secret that Will has a crush on Britney but he has never been able to get close to her because she was dating NSync star Justin Timberlake.

Britney and Justin broke up just last month. Could Ms Spears be on the rebound?

We hope for William that this isn't a publicity stunt. It could be said that Britney has had a lot of bad publicity lately.

Her new restaurant, which opened just last week, has given five people food poisoning already.

From an inside source, we learnt that Britney and Will have been on a string of dates since Britney has been in London.

Our photographer spotted them kissing at *The Ivy*. It has also been said that Britney took a liking to Will in 1998 when she first met him.

Britney broke up with Justin over his antics with model, Vicki.

She has been the *Queen of Pop* for five years now, since the tender age of sixteen.

How would you feel about an American being queen of England?

Email us at will4britney@hotmail.com.

Vicki Fitzsimons (14)
Coloma Convent Girls' School, Surrey

MYTHS AND LEGENDS

Have you ever heard of the Fethreds? That's not a surprise. That is because there is only one left in the whole world.

A single Fethrod has an enormous nose with big black nostrils. It also has small yellow duck's feet and wings, although it cannot fly. The rest of its body is bright green and it has pink eyes. To complete this strange sight, the Fethreds have huge afro hair, black in colour. The Fethreds live in colonies in underground caves.

The Fethreds lived 2006 years ago in Afghanistan. The Afghanis and the Fethreds had lived together reasonably well, but when the Afghanis' food started to run out, the Fethreds started to worry.

The Afghanis used to eat the eyes of pink sheep. These animals were very clever and they realised that if they didn't want to become extinct, they had to escape and quickly. The Afghanis had to eat, so they started hunting the Fethreds. Unlike the pink sheep, Fethreds are incredibly stupid, as well as being incredibly fat. They couldn't escape from the Afghanis, so very slowly, they began to dwindle in numbers.

I am the last Fethrod alive in the whole world. I am very old and will probably die soon, leaving this amazing colony of animals as a little-known memory. I couldn't do that, so I decided to tell others my story of our extinction. So if anyone else asks you if you have ever heard of the Fethreds, tell them you have.

Emily McDonald (13)
Coloma Convent Girls' School, Surrey

RETURN

She looked at the mysterious house. It was big, musty and silent. There was a footpath coated in glittering snow. A distinctive gnome appeared to stare at her, grinning, mocking. She walked into the garden nevertheless. Her clothes smelt, her face was muddy and unwashed, covered with long, wavy blonde hair, dull with neglect.

A tear escaped her eye and crystallised in the cool air upon her cheek. She took a swift step forwards, leaving a deeply engraved footprint in the snow, then another, then she stopped, both feet firmly fixed to the ground. With both eyes fixed at the familiar red door, she gasped suddenly, her nerves getting the better of her.

Her fear soon vanished. She stepped forwards again. The door was nearer to her now. She moved closer, crushing the snow beneath her feet. She looked above the door, through a window at a lonely, desperately silent room. It was pink, surrounded with pretty bows. She could see the bed. A doll lay on it, yet no girl was there playing with the doll and wearing the bows. She knew where that girl was . . .

Then she knocked the door, three times, then she waited. Her anger was fierce, hungry for revenge. The red door creaked open.
'Kitty!' gasped a middle-aged woman.
'Mum,' she hissed, 'I forgot to say goodbye.' Then she walked away. Revenge had been sweet, she thought, as her mum called out for her.

Sophie Fenlon (13)
Coloma Convent Girls' School, Surrey

THE BEST FAIRY IN THE WORLD

There was once a fairy called Indigo, she lived in a forest called Rose Forest. It was beautiful there because that's where all the fairies lived, in fact, they were all tooth fairies. There was a waterfall made of gold where all the coins came from, to be put under the pillows of little children. Fairies would paint rainbows in the sky and the leaves in autumn. When it snowed they put frost on the windows and created different patterns in the snow.

Indigo was a very clumsy fairy and wasn't good at doing all the things the other fairies did. When she painted rainbows the colours would always run together. When she painted the leaves, instead of doing them red and orange she did them pink and blue and when she did frost on the window they would always lack detail, compared to the other fairies.

Well, one day Indigo was up in the sky looking down on the world when she saw a boy crying. She went down and read his thoughts. He was upset because his tooth wouldn't fall out. Indigo put him to sleep with her magic fairy dust and pulled the tooth out for him. That night she went and gave the boy money.

The fairies would often laugh at Indigo because she never got anything right but she had made the boy happy so they decided to give her another chance. She soon became the best tooth fairy in the world.

Joanne Acott (13)
Coloma Convent Girls' School, Surrey

A DAY IN THE LIFE OF DR LOUISE WHITE

'Okay, what've I got?'
'Fourteen-year-old with leukaemia. Curtain 5.'
Dr White went in to talk to Helen, her patient.
'No thank you Dr White.'
'What do you mean? It's your chemo.'
'No more drugs. I can't take it any more. Just let me go naturally. No more junk pumping through my blood.'
'Oh Helen, I know it's tough but you have to stick with it. You'll get better, I promise. I know you feel awful and sometimes you don't have the energy to go on, but it's worth it, I know it is.'

Dr White sat with Helen for ninety minutes, talking about life and death and she persuaded her patient to stick with the chemo and to fight the cancer. These were the moments she loved, when she felt she was really making a difference, really helping people. Being a doctor was difficult and sometimes she felt like she just couldn't do it any more. But she did, she still did it every day. And when Helen had looked up at her and whispered, 'Thank you Dr White,' she knew she had been right.

She walked into curtain 5 with Helen's lunch and found her dead body hanging from the ceiling. So the chemo wires really did kill her after all. A tear slipped slowly down the doctor's cheek.

Lucy Coley (13)
Coloma Convent Girls' School, Surrey

THE BEAUTY

Deep in the woods, so deep it could not be found, lived a graceful, snow-white creature. Its fur looked soft and silky and was one of its best features. As it stood proud, it slowly sat down. The two front hooves were warmed by the comfy chest. It lay its head down to sleep, peaceful and at rest. Trickles of dew fell from the green leaves, hanging onto the trees above. As it hit against the body of the creature, it slowly slid off. Upon the creatures head was a horn, stronger than any other, more amazing and attractive too. You could not compare this horn to the tusk of an elephant, for the creature it was upon was a unicorn.

The unicorn always seemed to be tired, weary and breathless. She was also lonely and sad. She wanted to discover the wonders of the woods, to see if she could find another one of her kind. She had always wanted to do this in her mind.

One morning she set off. The sky was a delight, the sun, red, rising through the trees and shining so bright. The unicorn galloped off feeling the lovely, cool, fresh breeze running through her mane. The unicorn ran for days on end, searching for a newborn friend. One day she saw a beautiful sight through the trees. He really enjoyed to amuse and please her. They settled in the woods, living happily ever after, as graceful unicorns should.

Mary-Antoinette Fernandes (13)
Coloma Convent Girls' School, Surrey

ABIGAL WOOD

In Abigal Wood lies the land of the fairies. It is a magical and mystical place, that no human eye can see. It is hidden in the heart of the waterfall, between the rocks and the trees. And here live the fairies, all bright and full of joy, for today is a special day for all the girls and boys. Today is the fairy ball, a day off from the fairy school. A time when fairies can sing and laugh whilst dancing to the fairies' dance. But here sits Glitter, all alone, with no one to take her hand. She is desperate to dance along to the joyous fairy band. Then up pops Dewdrop, a handsome, dashing figure, in front of Glitter's sight. She hesitates a moment and then sits down in fright.

'What if he doesn't want to, what if he doesn't like me?' she sighs. She did not notice Dewdrop come to her side.

'Would you like a dance?' he said, 'I'd be honoured if you will!'

'Of course I would, and thank you,' she said as she sprang up off the hill. They danced all night in the light of the moon, in hope that the moment was not to end soon.

In Abigal Wood lies the land of the fairies. It is a magical and mystical place, that no human eye can see. This is where the fairies live in peace and harmony.

Jade Persaud-Walters (13)
Coloma Convent Girls' School, Surrey

A SHORT STORY

How could this happen to me? My heart was pounding, me of all people, I was too young to go. I was scared, I didn't want to leave. Cold sweat ran down my neck as I came to terms with what was going on. I wondered to myself, how could something so small grow and take me away? A warm hand was placed on my shoulder but it was trembling with fear. 'This will only make us stronger,' it mumbled. But I knew it would break my family.

That night, when my mum told the whole story to the family, my two brothers just sat there in silence and worst of all, my dad began to cry. I had never seen my dad cry before. How could I leave them? My family would just fall apart and it would be all my fault. I knew I only had a couple of days left, so I just had to do one last thing before I went.

I took my bike down to the river. It was so peaceful there. The sunlight bounced off the water and it seemed to wink at you as it twinkled. I often come down here to clear my head and today I really needed to.

As I sat there I thought of my parents and brothers and their characteristics and realised that what my mum said at the doctor's was true, that this would only make us stronger.

As I made my way home I knew I could leave in peace.

Emily Keegan (13)
Coloma Convent Girls' School, Surrey

MOVING HOUSE

It was Friday 13th July. It was a warm day and I was packing the last box of my stuff. I wrote my name and shook to think I was moving away from the house I was literally born in! I didn't want to move to Nightmare Street, especially to number 13. Rumours have it that it's haunted and that everyone that has moved in died on the second day. I don't usually listen to rumours and I didn't believe in Friday the 13th, until that very day.

The removal van had these razor-sharp teeth, it was roaring to go. The van was loaded and we set off. The van pulled to a sudden halt. It screeched, just like it was screaming. We were now outside my home. The removal men dumped our bags on the street and drove off in a hurry. My mum walked forward with our stuff and smiled. I knew that she was frightened and did believe the rumours, but I didn't want to say anything. 'Right, come on everyone, bring the stuff in!'

The night passed and the morning came. I turned on the TV and it said, 'Hello, welcome to CBBC, it's Friday morning and we've received some emails.' How could that be? The day strolled on and it was evening. My family and I were sat at dinner. We heard a voice whisper in the distance, 'You're going to die!' The floor collapsed and we never saw day again.

Kirsty Taylor (13)
Coloma Convent Girls' School, Surrey

A DAY IN THE LIFE OF AN AFRICAN SLAVE

I woke up on a cold, damp floor, with the sun shining brightly on my face, so brightly that I had to shield my eyes. I stood up with a stiff back and I put on my tatty, ripped shirt.

I walked out of my tiny home and rushed to the fields to work. A guard screamed at me to hurry up and I had to rush to join my other worker friends. The sun beamed down on my back so strong that it stung. The sweat on my brow trickled down my face like a stream and my hands were as red as tomatoes.

The long hours of the day pass slowly and during this time we have breaks to watch those who have tried to run away or disobeyed theirs masters, getting whipped. Their screams are painful and the slap of the whip, strong and sharp. the guards see this as a sport. They are mean and treat us like animals. It is very late when we manage to get to sleep but we cheer ourselves up when we have religious ceremonies, with laughter, singing and dancing. Every day is the same, long and hard. Will this pain ever end, will we have justice?

Jemima McWilliams (13)
Coloma Convent Girls' School, Surrey

A DAY IN THE LIFE OF DAVID BECKHAM

Have you ever wondered what it would be like to be a model, someone famous or a star? Well the truth is that it's not that different to our lives!

David woke that morning tired and feeling rough. Brooklyn had kept him up most of the night again. It felt so quiet without his wife there. She'd been called out to a photo shoot in Paris the night before.

Lonely, David reached into his fridge and poured himself some milk. He really wasn't in the mood for football today, but the team were counting on him. He gobbled down his breakfast, had a quick wash and threw on some joggers.

The doorbell rang. It was Victoria's mum, she'd come to look after Brooklyn while David was playing football.
'Where is he?' she asked. The toddler came bounding down the stairs in his Burberry trousers and matching top and cap.
'Really David, you and Vicky spoil him,' said Brooklyn's grandmother laughing.
'Bye Daddy!' cried Brooklyn.
'Bye mate, see you later!' And with that David took off on his way to work.

David's journey home seemed like ages. He was so tired. When he got out of his car and put the key in the lock, he muttered, 'It's a hard life being famous!'

Chloe McDonagh (13)
Coloma Convent Girls' School, Surrey

THE DEATH DEVOURER - CREATURE INSIDE THE MYTHICAL FOREST

The story goes . . . every time it is a full moon and the owls hoot, a gate opens up, although it's not a normal gate but a pathway to a whole new world. This mysterious gate opens into forest that only appears at night. Anyone who is sensible or knows about the Forest of Death, which no one lives in, well except for one person who no one talks about, does not dare enter.

Many kids have been lost or never seen again after being tempted by the lure of the gate. The parents think they have been abducted by the perils that lurk in society but there is more to it than meets the eye.

There was talk a long time ago about a reckless teenage boy who went to the Forest of Gloom, where his life would ultimately end. Everything had died in the forest. He trod over the dead life and saw that it was as dry as a barren desert.

Suddenly he heard noises. The creature came closer and closer. Screams could be heard amidst the sounds of this starry night. The creature was fifty times the size of him, it was the worst sight the boy had ever seen. The gate suddenly closed and the boy vanished, never to be seen again.

There was a tall, dark figure standing in front of the gate gleaming in the moonlight. He did not help the boy, he just told the story and watched. But why was he there every time a child went into the forest, why?

Rachel Cable (13)
Coloma Convent Girls' School, Surrey

A Day In The Life Of A Rich Lady After World War II

Dear Diary,

At 7am I woke up. My servants were filling a bath for me. I was excited as I was going to buy a new hat that I had seen in the window the other day when I was in town.

After my bath I had to go to the newsagents to buy the Daily Sketch. The main headline was *At Last The War Is Over!* We lived in the country so it didn't affect us that much, except we had all the evacuees coming to stay with people in the countryside, but I didn't get any.

I took a long stroll in the park. I sat down on a bench while I read the newspaper. I thought to myself that Hitler was a madman and they should lock him up and throw away the key.

It was about lunchtime so I decided to make my way back to the house for tea. I went home and my husband was waiting for me.
He said, 'Come on, where have you been?'
'Oh, I just went for a stroll in the park,' I replied as he poured me a cup of tea, warm from the pot.
After I finished drinking my tea we were off to the hat shop in town. On our way we could see the distraction and sadness the war brought to some of the people who it had affected.

When we arrived at the shop I could see the hat gleaming at me. I went in and tried it on. It fitted perfectly.

Jessica Mitchell (13)
Coloma Convent Girls' School, Surrey

JUST ANOTHER SLAVE STORY

Another hot, sunny day in Mississippi. Collette was out on the plantation farm picking cotton, just like she always had for the last thirteen years. She started work at 6am and finished at 10pm. She did not have a break in-between.
Mr Cook, the overseer always said, 'The day you get a break is the day I die, now get back to work!'

Collette always daydreamed of her family, she remembered it like yesterday. She led her seven children to the auction block, knowing that this was going to be goodbye. The children were sold to a slave-trader, while she was bought by another.

She'd wrung her hands in anguish and exclaimed, 'Gone, all gone! Why doesn't God kill me?' In less than 24 hours she had gone from being a mother of seven to a broken-hearted woman who had lost the will to live.

Mr Cook was watching Collette, as a predator awaits its prey. Suddenly he violently slammed her on the floor while reaching up her dress. Collette fought back until he took his last breath and departed from this Earth. Fleeing from the scene she ran into the night, running away from bondage and captivity towards freedom and her children.

Mayowa Odusote (13)
Connaught School For Girls, London

A DAY IN THE LIFE OF A CLASSROOM CHAIR

I mean what have I ever done? All I ever do in life is sit there. Occasionally I get moved but that's it.

I remember in the good old days, standing in the factory, all of us could hardly wait to be sent to a school and be used. Of course that's before I ever knew what classroom life was like. I remember thinking just the night before I was about to be sent to a classroom, these are gonna be the best days of my life. I mean back then I was clean, spotless and nothing was broken. I was perfect. If you look at me now, well, that's a completely different story. Now there's not even one word that would compliment me nicely.

I'm in Ms Rauf's class and boy has she got a load of weirdoes! Now one girl is what I would call large. When she comes into the classroom she sits her great behind down and wriggles around until she's comfy. Now this wouldn't be so bad if once she'd get comfy she would stay there. But all the way through the lesson, through that whole one hour, she wriggles this way, then that way and once she's started there's no stopping her. Then as if this wasn't bad enough, she comes out with, 'This chair's broke, look at it,' she says, once she notices her friends are there.

Now this next one, she really is the worst of them all. She always comes and sits on me. This girl, she doesn't wriggle around or do graffiti on me. She's not fat, surprisingly, with the amount she eats. Whenever she comes in the classroom she sits herself down on me. When the class is set work she starts working. Now hearing all this you must be thinking, what is my problem with her? As soon as the teacher stops watching, that's when she gets her things out. First she gets out a small plastic bag, out of this she takes some crackers. Unfortunately all the crumbs fall onto me. She then gets out her carton of orange juice to rinse down the taste of the crackers. Of course, a bit of juice drips onto me, leaving a wet, sticky patch. Then, just as she's finished she sees the teacher coming, so she starts sweeping off the crumbs, as though nothing's happened. She does this every lesson. It's tedious watching her do the same things over and over again.

Finally the year is drawing to an end. There's only a couple of days to go until the summer holidays. Ms Rauf is making the pupils take down all the posters. Oh no, what's that tall girl doing with me? Oh, this really is the limit. She's standing on me so she can reach a poster on the wall. As if she isn't tall enough already. This is getting too much for my old legs. All of a sudden one of my legs breaks off the chair.

Well, I've been taken out of the classroom. I think they're going to throw me away. Oh well, a new adventure starts here!

Charlotte Braithwaite (13)
Connaught School For Girls, London

THE OLD LADY AT KHUMALI

Lalitlia was the most kind-hearted girl in the Khumali village. She lived with her mother, father and sister. Lalitlia's father was the chief of the Khumali village so everyone respected her family. Everybody liked Lalitlia because she was so kind, but unlike Lalitlia, Rebecca her sister, was cruel and conceited.

Although Lalitlia had a great family, she was always sad because her sister Rebecca was so selfish and she always broke Lalitlia's dolls. One day when Lalitlia was at the river washing her clothes, an old lady with blisters all over her body came up to Lalitlia and asked her to wash her body. Although the lady looked disgusting, Lalitlia felt sorry for her and because Lalitlia was so kind-hearted, she agreed. She washed her and the old lady invited her to her home. Lalitlia was grateful and agreed to go.

When they got to the old lady's house, the old lady gave Lalitlia a plate with snails, ants and worms. Lalitlia figured that it was the only food the woman had. She did not want to be ungrateful or make the lady feel bad so she just ate it.

The woman was overwhelmed with Lalitlia's kindness and told Lalitlia that she would give her anything she wanted. Lalitlia was puzzled. the old lady suddenly turned into a beautiful princess.

The princess began to explain that she changed into an old lady with blisters and asked people to wash her so that she could see how kind people were. She went on to say that when Lalitlia agreed to wash her and eat her food she was surprised because Lalitlia was the first person to agree. The princess told Lalitlia that she was flattered by her kindness, so she decided to give Lalitlia anything she wanted.

Lalitlia was happy and she asked for all the toys a girl could want. The princess then told her that her presents would be waiting for her at home in her room. Lalitlia was very grateful and she thanked the princess. The princess told Lalitlia not to tell anyone who she was and said whoever asked her where she got her presents, she should say an old lady I washed gave them to me.

When she got home her sister asked her how and where she got her toys. Lalitlia told her that she washed an old lady at the river and the old lady gave her the toys.

Rebecca left the house and went to the river. When she got there she found the old lady sitting by the river. The old lady asked Rebecca to wash her. Rebecca then showed a disgusting face, then she agreed. When she'd washed the old lady, she was invited to the old lady's house. When she got there she was given the same food Lalitlia got. She began to make disgusting comments and refused to eat the food. The old lady was angered by this so she cast a spell on Rebecca and sent her home.

When she got home everyone was saying that Rebecca was stinking. Rebecca went and took a bath. But when she got out she was still stinking. For a week people were avoiding Rebecca. No one could stand Rebecca's smell any more so they went and complained to the chief (Rebecca's dad). The chief was unhappy but everyone demanded that Rebecca should be sent out of the Khumali village. Rebecca was sent far away.

No one has seen Rebecca since, but it is said that she still walks around the Khumali forest in search of her village.

As for the old lady (princess), legends say that she still sits by the Khumali river waiting to ask someone to wash her.

Sibongile Natasha Tsoka (13)
Connaught School For Girls, London

A DAY IN THE LIFE OF A PEN

Hey, hey you, don't take my feathers off my beautiful body. Oh no someone help me, I think she's going to bite my top off. Phew, that was so close. Can you just imagine what I would look like without my purple, shiny, glittering feathers? I would look awful, like I have no clothes.

Oh no I'm going in her mouth, what shall I do?
All my feathers are wet now and I feel horrible and you'll never guess what. Her breath stinks. Has anyone got a Tictac for this girl, she needs it as I might die in here.

Guess what? Her teeth are dirty too, has she never heard of a toothbrush and toothpaste? That's why it stinks in here. There she goes again chewing on my feathers, I just can't stop her. Good, I am out of her mouth now, what a relief. *I feel sick!* And you will never guess what, she has just put me up her nose and I've got bogey on my feathers.

Do you know how long it's going to take me to clean my feathers after what she's done to them? I may have no feathers left at the end. Yes, one more word and my ink's finished, living with this girl has been like Hell. Now she's screwing my top off. There she goes changing my ink and you know what from the first day I've lived with her it's been like this ever since.

Tashbila Salamut (13)
Connaught School For Girls, London

THE LEGEND OF THE BLACK GRIFFIN

Do we know every animal in the world? This legend began in Egypt. They had a good god called Horus - God of Light. There was a bad god named Anubis - God of Death.

Anubis and his followers reigned terror to all who disobeyed him to do bad deeds, but Horus planned in secret to defend the good people. He created a good omen called the Black Griffin.

The Griffin had a lion's body, huge birds' wings and a big eagle's head. The Griffin was gigantic. It had black feathers, golden eyes, claws, wings and a golden feather on its head. It looked like an evil omen. The Black Griffin was hidden in a tomb and was told to awaken if anything terrible happened.

The worst terror came one night. Anubis was putting innocent people to death. The Black Griffin rose from the tomb, blowing the mightiest wind, which killed many of Anubis' followers; the others heard a sweet screech that made them melt into ooze. Anubis rose from the underworld and tried to cast a mighty death spell on the Black Griffin but it rebounded, hit Anubis and drained his dark powers. Horus commanded the Black Griffin to use its golden feather to kill Anubis. Suddenly the sun began to shine through darkness and hit the Black Griffin's golden feather; making a beam of white and gold light that killed Anubis.

The Black Griffin was the guardian of Egypt. Now we know we don't know every animal in the world!

Kausar Bibi Torabally (13)
Connaught School For Girls, London

ACNE AARON

It was a cold, dark night. The wind was howling at the moon. Acne Aaron was walking home from a hard day's work. Out of the shadows a mysterious man popped out, dropped a box and note in Aaron's hand. Before Aaron could say anything, the man vanished. He ran home and read the note. It said, 'Desperate? Then use this acne cream and your face will clear up'.

Aaron covered his whole face with the acne cream. He went into a sweet slumber; he hadn't slept in days for he recapped on all the teasing that he encountered.

He woke up in the morning and looked in the mirror. His skin was shiny and soft with no spots visible. For once in his life he looked handsome, like a whole new person.

He went to work and all the women flirted with him, when they came to order at McDonald's. He was ecstatic. A woman was talking to him when a horn pierced through his forehead. The pain made him scream and the woman ran off. He ran into the bathroom and looked in the mirror and fainted due to the ugly sight.

Just then the mysterious man popped in and saw the state Aaron was in. He took Aaron into his laboratory and found a cure. He used the formula and acne Aaron was himself once again, but it was too late. Aaron's body was too weak with no energy to keep his eyes open and to breathe . . .

Jasmine Patel (14)
Connaught School For Girls, London

A DAY IN THE LIFE OF A DESK!

Hey you! Stop writing on me you bully. I'm a desk not a piece of paper. What are you doing now? Just because the teacher has gone out of the classroom, doesn't give you permission to start jumping on me!

At last the bell has gone which means this classroom will be empty for about fifteen minutes. Now it's quiet in here, I can have a chat with my friend next to me and catch up on all the gossip.

'Hey Sandy, did you know that desk over there has about 33 pieces of gum stuck underneath it?'
'That's nothing, I have about 56 pieces stuck under me. Oh yeah, and just look at all this writing all over me. I've got things written on me like 'Joey was 'ere', 'school sucks' and I even know who fancies who!'
'Don't worry Sandy, they will all come off tomorrow.'
'What do you mean these will be coming off? They can't come off. Some of the kids write with permanent pens and even engrave their names into me.'
'Come on Sandy, haven't you ever heard of the man who comes round every two years with the monster called 'the sander'? He'll soon get rid of them.'

Oh well, there goes the bell. That's the end of break time. Soon there will be another load of noisy kids in here!

What a life!

April Macpherson (13)
Connaught School For Girls, London

THE BRANTWATU MYTH

Since anyone can remember the hideous Brantwatu monster has forever been lurking beneath the Atlantic Ocean. The Brazilian villagers would always get a visit from this strange, mysterious creature. Every visit that the Brazilians received a young child would always go missing. The only time a little child wouldn't disappear is when the blood of a virgin was put on the tongue of an ugly toad, then sacrificed at twelve o'clock midnight.

The villagers seemed to be having a great deal of trouble providing this request for the Brantwatu monster, as there weren't a great number of virgins in the village. The villagers began to think of new sacrifices; but none of them seemed to work until one day, after a lot of research, a young boy discovered that the Brantwatu monster loved fresh blood. Therefore he told all the village people to try a new sacrifice, which was, a young fish was to be fried in the blood of a newborn lamb, then it was to be sacrificed at the door of everyone's house.

This seemed to work and little by little the missing children began to reappear. Yet while the children were reappearing, the parents seemed to be miraculously vanishing. At first the children were rather worried about their missing parents, but then they began to realise the advantages of not having their parents around. They decided not to do anything about it for the moment, instead they relaxed and enjoyed their few moments of freedom.

Dorcas Kissi (13)
Connaught School For Girls, London

A DAY IN THE LIFE OF A . . .

'Hi everybody. Oh my gosh, why is it so dark in here? Hello, is anybody listening?'

'Quiet! You're disturbing everyone and who are you?'

'I'm really sorry but I'm not used to this. I'm just a pencil who's been thrown into this dark case. It's really hard to breathe.'

'I know I was in the same position once . . . still am.'

I was tall, lovely and sharp but one day someone pressed me really hard against the desk and ouch! That really hurt. All of a sudden I was carried over to something fat and round and was squashed into the mouth of a beast called a *sharpener.*

I still remember being tortured. I went to sleep hoping that this was a nightmare and I would wake up a brand new pencil again. But the next morning I awoke looking old and shrunken.

I felt embarrassed to be taken out but didn't have a choice. There I was at an upright position ready to be used. Left to right, left to right . . . I carried on.

Every so often there was a slight pause, in which I felt my head being chewed. I realised I was experiencing the inside of someone's mouth. Since then I've hidden at the bottom and shiver when I see light.

'But I don't want to be used, help me.'

'I would if I could but these giants just won't understand us. I think it's your turn now. Good luck!'

Left to right, left to right . . .

Mavish Mahmood (13)
Connaught School For Girls, London

A DAY IN THE LIFE OF A CHAIR

Here I am alone in an empty classroom doing nothing. Wait a minute! I can hear people. Oh no, it's the children waiting for their next lesson. Here they come.

You'll never guess what happened yesterday. Some boy called Thomas farted in my face. I was five seconds away from death because of the smell, when suddenly he stood up. Gosh, I've never felt the air smell that good. I thought it was over when he came back and sat on my face with a thump.

Today it didn't seem that Thomas was here because he wasn't in the classroom, but the girl who sat next to him was. Her name was Danielle. She is very thin and light. I don't mind if she sits on me, but not Thomas. I am a bit old to be sat on now. My legs are bent and are about to break. Nobody cares about me and they don't even know that I'm about to break. I thought that Thomas wasn't here, but I thought wrong, he is here. He's always late for lessons, that's alright, then he gets less time to sit on me.

Phew, there's only five minutes left until the lesson finishes, but I think there's only five seconds left for me to break. 5, 4, 3, 2 . . .

Aqsa Farman (13)
Connaught School For Girls, London

A Day In The Life Of A Lice

'Yuck, yuck, ugh!'
'She's got nits. Look, it's moving!'
'Look, it's all brown and look how big it is!'
'Oh my goodness! It's crawling down.'
'Ugh . . . it's jumped in Amber's hair!'
'Lice, lice, lice, Amber's got lice,' shouted the kids.
'What? Lice!'

'Lice, why are they calling me lice?'
'I'm Freddy.'
'Oh my gosh, this is the cleanest head I've ever been in.'
'Yeap, this is the life, no dandruff, no white bits, no flaky scalp.'
'So where shall I lay my eggs then?'

'Amber . . . look . . . in your . . .'
'No don't tell her, it's her problem she's got lice!'

'They're talking about me again, but why? Why are they calling me nits and lice? I just don't get it! For goodness sake, I'm Freddy.'

'Amber, look there's a nit in your hair.'
'Argh . . . ouch! Where? Get it out!'
'I'm homeless, homeless I tell you! Nooo! I can't go anywhere.'

'Yuck, kill the lice. Step on it Amber.'

'Ooh, the big foot's coming down on me, I better run fast.'
'I missed it, damn! It got away, that stupid thing.'

'Yes saved, thank goodness!'
'So now where shall I go? I can't find anyone's hair.'
'Wow! There's a boy lying on the floor, my perfect chance. Come on, I can do it. Come on. No, he's getting up. Nearly there. Yes, made it.'

'Jimmy, yucky, you've got something in you hair, and it's moving!'
'Nooo!'

Noreen Ahmed (13)
Connaught School For Girls, London

A DAY IN THE LIFE OF A TRAMP

Money, money, I need money. I sit on the streets begging just like I have been doing for the past ten years, however, no one is coming. I need a fag, I need a drink and for once I feel like I need to brush my teeth.

When those people in uniforms come round asking me about my life story, what do they expect me to say apart from my ma died when I was eleven and then my pops chucked me out when I was sixteen and I've been living the hard way ever since.

I don't have no family and no friends; they're all dead to me - in the past, gone!

I have tried making friends but then again no one wants to know me. They just see me as a loser sitting on the streets begging for money. I may beg on the streets but I'm not a loser. I'm just like you, a person. I have feelings and I suppose I am dirty and unclean, but I am still a human being.

I have tried hostels and other places, but they don't really care, they just try to make as much money as they can by trying to be nice to us.

Today I walked into a café; a few people took one look at me and then walked out, the rest just held their noses until I'd gone. But they will see one day I'm going to be someone and I won't take money for granted.

Paula Agyemang-Duah (13)
Connaught School For Girls, London

A Day In The Life Of A Pencil

All alone in the pencil case with some colours that won't shut up. Just as I am about to drop off I am picked up and used without any permission. They slam me on the table making my lead break, then they use a sharp blade to bring the lead back up. (If I reported them to the police it would be called attempted murder!) After all that, I am then again thrown on the floor and when they reach down to get me they start huffing and puffing like it's my fault. Then, to top it all off, the cycle happens again and again until there's nothing left of me. They just think I am their property and I don't have feelings, but deep down inside my lead, it really hurts. They have even given my rear end a name, 'the rubber'. Surely you know pen and paper are enemies but that doesn't stop the hooligans. We also have copycats called 'the pens'.

I think I deserve a nice tin home with a picture of me in front, with no colours to annoy me. I would put a lock on it so I wouldn't get abused. Oh well, my dream will come true one day.

Cherrelle Campbell (13)
Connaught School For Girls, London

CREEK'S CHALLENGE

Mykanos is a very greedy person and does not think of other people. He only cares about himself and what he is going to have for his next meal.

Creek, king of Athens, has just come back from visiting Africa. While he was in Africa he saw lots of people who didn't have enough to eat.

When he came home he called Mykanos to come and see him. He told him about the people of Africa and said, 'Instead of thinking about yourself, you can go and help the people of Africa.'
'Why should I go and why do they need help anyway?' Creek told him about how hungry they were and how they didn't have any food. 'What no food! I can't go somewhere where there is no food.'

Creek was not very happy with Mykanos and told him that he was being set a challenge to go to help these people grow some food so that they would not starve. Mykanos said, 'Well, how will I get to Africa?' Creek gave him a boat to get there.

He went to Africa and found a little hut to live in. He was very hungry after his journey and asked one of the local people where he could get some food for his dinner and they told him that there wasn't any food. With that he realised how very, very hungry he was and how hungry all the people of Africa were, and he became very hungry indeed.

His anger grew as well. He was angry with Creek, but decided that he must do something to get food. He needed some help though. He had seen monkeys and birds around his hut looking for food. He used his supernatural powers to talk to them and he decided to use them. He asked them all to go and get as many seeds as they could find, which they did.

He sowed the seeds and commanded the clouds to come so he could water the seeds. He didn't want small clouds, as they didn't bring rain. He didn't want huge thunder clouds with heavy rain, as they would wash the seeds away. Instead he made it rain gently all day.

He tended the ground each day and soon saw some shoots coming through. However, they needed some sun for the plants to grow big and healthy, so he made a deal with the sun and the rain and made it rain all night and the sun to shine all day. The crops soon grew and the people soon had grain to make bread, oats to make porridge and vegetables to give them vitamins. The people became stronger and were able to grow their own crops.

Once he saw that they were happy and healthy, he ate enough to get him back to Athens, bailed out his boat, which was full of rainwater, and went back to Athens to tell Creek what he had done.

Creek saw him coming and asked if he had completed his challenge, thinking that he hadn't. Mykanos answered proudly that he had and explained how, 'Once I saw the people could feed themselves again I returned.' Creek then asked what Mykanos had learnt from his challenge. He replied, 'I learnt not to think about myself all the time and that I should share things with other people, especially food!'

The African people can now live normal lives because they are stronger, healthier and a lot happier.

Gloucester Class, Year 7
Dorton House School, Kent

THE SECRET GARDEN

On a hot summer's evening, I went to bed feeling really sticky. I twisted and turned and when I finally got comfy, I fell into a deep sleep and started to dream. At first it was misty and as I walked through the mist I went into, what seemed to me, to be a forest. I came to a clearing and stopped suddenly. I was speechless, I could not believe my eyes. It was beautiful, lots and lots of wonderful colours and different sizes and shapes of flowers and plants. There were roses and daffodils, also lemon trees and orange trees. The smell was sensational, the sweet scent of the perfumed roses and daffodils filled the air.

I took a deep breath in and my lungs filled with fresh air and I felt great, as if I had left Earth and gone up into Heaven for a while. When I came back into reality, I saw a swing. It looked as if it had been there for ages and it put a rather nice look to the garden.

There were rose petals on the luscious green grass. I lay down in them and fell asleep, when I woke up I found myself back in my bed again. I remembered what had happened and whenever I am sad or lonely I think about the dream I had in the secret garden.

Anna Fearnley (14)
Gads Hill School, Kent

THE SHIP OF DREAMS

Edward adjusted his bow tie and pulled on his dinner jacket. After a small number of days commanding the magnificent ship, which was heading for America, he had been invited to join other first class guests for evening supper.

A doorman, his white gloves as pure as angels, held the pine door open for Edward, bowing as he did so. An overwhelming burst of sound dispersed into the air. Endless loquacious talk, boastful and meaningless gestures.

Edward entered the room, attracting the attention of the guests who crowded into the exorbitant dining hall. Table upon table flashed with wine glasses, twinkling like stars which decorated the night sky. Unhabituated china plates were laid out, waiting to be used. Sparkling chandeliers plunged from the ceiling. Edward was seated; an array of luminous cutlery had been placed before him. His guests arranged themselves at the table. Another revolution of conversation spread.

The women who joined Edward displayed a magnificent rainbow of colour in their evening gowns. Layer upon layer of silky material tumbled to the ground, tightened corsets compressed their bodies. Like opposing armies, the women tried to win over Edward with their private speech.

'I simply *adore* the ship!' one shrilled.
'Exquisite decor! Imaginative arrangement of rooms!' another cried.

Edward soaked up the attention, sipping his wine and showing vague interest to the people who joined him.

Robyn Cordes (14)
Glenthorne High School, Surrey

A Day In The Life Of A Monkey In A Zoo

Oh no, not another open day! It feels like only yesterday when they were last poking and prodding me. I am Georgia, the only monkey here from Borneo, which means no friends and more poking.

I am awakened by my keeper, well the substitute, the new guy's a spotty 19-year-old who hasn't any consideration for anyone but himself. He takes me to the grounds where my cage will be open to the public. I can't be bothered to put up a fight anymore. I'd only die on my own, well that's what they tell me.

I feel scared inside my cage even though this isn't my first time. If only I could be taken away. Some of the people care, but not enough to adopt me or even come and visit me. The first time they released me from my cage was to a six-year-old who held me by the tail. I would have scratched her but I'd just be starved for it. Many others came and went: one even dropped me, but when the last person came I was glad, until they picked me up and cuddled me close.

The stroker was a gentle girl of about nine years. I clung to her and she was so kind. She smelt of honey and burnt toast but when her mother called her she had to go. She asked her mother if she could keep me but her mother just laughed and they walked away. I was back in my cage and when I was returned to the sanctuary I was given a few scraps of food. I cried silently at night but I knew that I should not be surprised. I am used to this, it's called 'my life'!

Phoebe Bukovenczki (11)
Hampstead School, London

THE DAY IN THE LIFE OF A COIN

Yesterday me and all my friends, Penny, Ten Pence, Crispy Note and 50p, were moving quite quickly, bouncing around. Then suddenly we stopped. A bright light was getting bigger and bigger, then a massive hand reached out and was coming towards us.

Before I knew it, all my friends were gone - Penny, Ten Pence and 50p. Only Crispy Note and me left. A long time had gone, I noticed that it was getting dark into the night. Then the massive hand reached into the pocket again, this time much slower.

We were so scared. Crispy Note wrapped around me, then we were lifted up by the hand, out of the dark, hot and squashed place. We both soon realised that we were with our good friend leather wallet, safe for the night!

In the morning we had just travelled to another black place, this time in a shop's cash machine, back with my very good friends.

Jordan Blake-Klein (11)
Hampstead School, London

A DAY IN THE LIFE OF A CAT

Life is hell! School, TV, eat, sleep. It's always the same boring routine. 'Dinner,' my mum calls, 'and hurry up, it's getting cold.'

I run downstairs. 'You said it was ready,' I shout irritably. It smells disgusting and looks it too. A huge bowl of thick stew has been put in front of me, everyone else starts eating whilst I sit staring at lumps of potatoes. I'd rather be eating cat food, at least it's meat. I look enviously at Syrup, our cat, who's gobbling down her food. *I wish I was a cat.* Suddenly I feel really tired and think it best to go and lie down - I'm just saying that, I don't want to eat the stew!

The next day I wake up and jump . . . I mean climb out of bed and go to look at my monstrous morning self in the mirror. I look in and the reflection staring back at me makes me jump. It's not me looking back at myself, it's a cat! The wish must have come true, or I'm dreaming! I try to shout, 'Mum!' but only a miaow comes out. I decide that if this is real then, hey, get used to it and if it's not, then enjoy it. I can't believe it, no school, no burnt toast!

Breakfast has been put out for me and I greedily take a huge mouthful, bleh! It's disgusting, it's salty and makes my mouth go dry. I spit it out and drink some water. Even Mum's stew was better than that. I see Syrup getting attention all the time, so I jump onto the table and start to purr.
'Bad cat, get outside.'

I get thrown outside and as if things can't get any worse, it starts pouring with rain. Life as a cat isn't so great after all. I suddenly feel really tired and fall asleep, not even noticing the rain.

The next day I wake up and run to look in the mirror. I'm back.
Life is great!

Sibyl Cooke Steed (13)
Hampstead School, London

A DAY IN THE LIFE OF JILL VALENTINE

My last hope! Why am I not dead like the rest of the people in the city? I was the one chosen by God to survive. Nemesis will strike again! My friend was first, I will be next. To Nemesis, surviving is not an option.

My name's Jill Valentine. I live in Manhattan. I work for the STARS police. Nemesis won't die, nothing would kill him. Armed with a machine-gun, a Magnum and a hand gun I must kill Nemesis, the vicious dogs, the hunters and the blood-sucking zombies All of them were affected by the T virus. Over 11,000 people have died, 3000 were evacuated. I hadn't found anybody alive yet. There's no hope for me, I will have an agonising death. They have taken everything from me, but I won't let them win. Not now.

My other friend, Brad, came in. 'Brad, I thought you were dead,' I said. 'I thought you were dead too, Jill,' he murmured.

Suddenly something jumped down from the roof of the police station and put a 5-metre hole through Brad's head. I screamed in horror. 'Nemesis STARS,' he shouted. I got my hand gun out and started shooting, no good, Nemesis was too powerful, the bullets just went through him. He fired two rockets at me. I dodged them. The man came out of nowhere with a sub machine-gun and started shooting. The bullets rebounded. He told me to hide. I did what I was told for once in my life.

Elliott Kenton (12)
Hampstead School, London

BACK IN TIME

12th June 1960

Dear Diary,

Hi, my name is Mark Twinick. I am 12¾ and I live with my mum and dad, oh yeah, and my older sister Julia.

Today was really eventful. I woke up to find my dog, Pepper, lying on my chest, licking my cheeks, then he turned around and blew off right in my face. It was gross. My mouth was open and everything!

I stumbled out of bed and looked in the mirror and saw that I had a great big spot on my chin, just my luck. I went downstairs for my breakfast only to find that my mum had bought me a new pair of trousers, they were red and purple and . . . wait for it . . . drum roll please . . . *they were flared!* When I saw them I smiled and said, 'Oh thanks Mum, they're great!' but really I wanted to be sick.

I felt thoroughly down until Shenall walked past the house, oh, she's beautiful! I'm in love, it has to be love, this can't be just a crush. I'm so glad I'm alive in the 60s, loads of discos and parties. I wonder what it will be like in the year 1997 or 2004? There will probably be flying cars and apes will rule the planet! Blimey, that's scary!

Sarah Nimmo (12)
Hampstead School, London

A DAY IN THE LIFE OF . . . A MIRROR

It seems weird, doesn't it? I am a mirror but I have never actually seen what I look like, I bet you've never thought about that before? Mirrors are very powerful, you know, we have a power hidden deep within. We can curse you, we can give you bad luck, seven years, seven long terrible years, and all you have to do is crack us. You might not believe me, you may have broken a fellow mirror before, and you're perfectly fine. This may be because your bad luck happens in a way that is unnoticed, or we might not even curse you, just the thought of you worrying about your bad luck satisfies us!

Well anyway, that's what I did after this little girl smashed *me,* she worried so, so much about it, but the thing that made me happy was that she jumped at every loud noise she heard! Her mother said it was ridiculous, but deep down I think she believed, because she tried to sell me, but she couldn't even give me away, who would want a broken mirror?

So now I spend my days up here in the attic, plotting my revenge, I should have given them all the worst luck I could conjure up. But there is no going back now, so I'll save it until the next person.

So the next time you pass a mirror, think about what I have told you today, you never know, it might change what happens next.

Rosie Bowman (12)
Hampstead School, London

MYTHS AND LEGENDS

Evangelos hung over the precipice of a huge, deep crack in the earth like a deep scratch made by some unearthly creature digging his fingernail deep into the ground. His face was tense and alert as he clung to the edge like a crouching tiger. Helena sat lazing on the other side in the sun, next to Evangelos' anxious-looking sister, Evandulina. 'I do hope he rescues us soon, Helena,' Evandulina murmured, peering into the depths of the murky darkness below, 'one would think that we will be stuck here forever.'

Helena smiled confidently and eyed her boyfriend flirtatiously as he reached for a glimmeringly sharp spear and flexed his muscles in doing so.
'Oh do stop worrying, Evandulina,' she smiled, flicking a lock of golden hair away from her face.

A low, supernatural groaning began to sound from the darkness. Evandulina gasped and began to move away from the sharp precipice, while Helena continued to laze in the sunshine.
'Evandulina, really. It's not up to us women, the men are the strong, powerful . . .' she began, but stopped in shock, her mouth still wide in mid-sentence.

A huge tree trunk-like neck towered in front of her. As her eyes moved upwards, she was frozen in shock at the horrifying sight that was before her. Glaring red eyes, crouched over slit nostrils. There was no ordinary mouth, only a hole with many sharp teeth, like rows of deadly daggers.

A glittering spear was flung against the terrible creature's skull, only to be tossed helplessly aside. The creature turned. A terrific crunching sound filled the air, Evandulina blinked and both her companions had gone. The monster began to retreat to its den. Within seconds, the creature fell to the side of the precipice with an enormous roar. A long, piercing scream followed by a crack filled the air. The monster, a spear piercing a lazy red eye, its neck broken, was dead.

Evandulina stood triumphantly gazing at the creature. 'Times are changing,' she said.

Shireen Qureshi (14)
Hampstead School, London

A DAY IN THE LIFE OF A CRISP PACKET

Last night was a very odd night. I spent it in a tree. Very weird, as I should be in the supermarket with all my mates, Salt and Pepper and Ready Salted. I'm Cheese and Onion, nice to meet you.

Being stuck up here all started yesterday morning. From what I remember I was in a dark, compact space with my mates, joking around and having a laugh, when suddenly, light was let in and a massive hand came at us and pushed us onto the top shelf along with the cakes. It was great being so high above the mad magazines and cruel chocolates.

It was soon over when a screaming child came in the shop and pulled me down and moaned to its mother till she bought me at 31p, yes, a worthless 31p. I mean, nothing! Anyway, the mother took me by the head and pulled, yes, pulled me open, oh, it hurt. Then she handed me over to the little crying child and he ate my insides. He munched and crunched and swallowed my insides up, then he . . . he dropped my empty, weightless body to the ground and I got swept away by the wind.

I was smashed into buildings, houses, cars, and then this big old tree and I couldn't move because the wind had gone off to blow some other poor soul into this tree.

I am just going to have to wait for the wind to come back, bye.

Sabina Brown (14)
Hampstead School, London

A Day In The Life Of A Pencil

I was suddenly roused from my rest by the bright sun through the window. The morning sun warmed me up. I heard footsteps faintly in the distance, a few seconds passed and the steps got louder as they reached the room I was in.

A young boy of three years dashed at me. He lifted me up from the table with his small fingers. He held me to a blank paper on a small desk. He held me stiffly and dragged my tail across the sheet. He continued with eagerness to use my tail to spell his name. I didn't mind as long as he didn't break off my tail after every letter.

After the writing session, he put me into a box and ran off down the corridor to his mother. By this time he'd broken my tail five times and I was upset at having grown shorter in minutes.

I soon learned that his friends were round to visit. They wanted to draw and write. Unfortunately I was the only pencil available so they all had to share me. By the time they've done their activities, I'll no longer exist (my poor tail having to be sharpened all the time). I dreaded this but luckily a few minutes later an adult voice called the children out of the room and they all came back with pencils in their hands.

I sat miserably through the session. No one wanted to use me any longer!

Iyanu Taiwo (14)
Hampstead School, London

THE DAY IN THE LIFE OF A PRISONER

Day 5:
I don't think that I can take it much longer in here. It's only stupid Day 5 and I still have to spend another 360 days in here. I'm going crazy. Every time I so much as think of where I am, all the blood rushes to my head, and my family - oh, how I miss them. All those happy days with my little baby, Annabel, she could always make me laugh - even if she'd done something cheeky, she could always make a little smile curl up in the corner of my mouth.

6.15am
Miss Bogtrotter comes storming in with a terrible cry coming from that revolting mouth in her poor excuse for a face. 'C'mon, gettup, yu' disgustin' piece o' filth.'

My head is spinning as I look up in a daze, wiping the drool from my mouth, I still 'adn't gotten used to the wake-up call.

6.45am
A sea of mindless prisoners pour into the dining room as the ancient cooks slap some slime and gruel onto our cheap plates. How I long for a big banana sandwich and a dollop of 'Double-Dutch Butterscotch' ice cream with fizzy cola sprinkles!

3.30pm
Time for another stomach-curling meal, after which, back to more slavery - digging in those mines, I can almost feel my lungs 'clogging up' - disgusting!

7.10pm
At last, something exciting has happened - Bone-crusher and Brain Fizzler had a fight! I know it's not very exciting but at the moment I'll enjoy anything!

9.30pm

It's lights out. I don't understand, everyone seems to cope fine but I'm slowly breaking. This place is devouring me bit by bit until I'll finally crack, and trust me - it won't be long.

Talisa Zampieri (12)
Hampstead School, London

A DAY IN THE LIFE OF ASHANTI

Oh no, I can't believe it's morning! Switch off the alarm clock at 6.30am. Today is going to be a long but wicked day. I'm appearing in *Party in the Park* this afternoon but I have loads to do before that.

Jump in the shower; I think I'll have scrambled egg and toast for breakfast and loads of orange juice. Oh drat, I'm late, I need to be at the studio by 8.30am to record the last track of my album.

I'll call a cab now. As I leave my apartment block, there are fans everywhere waiting for my autograph. I sign a few but have to dash to the cab.

At last I arrive at the studio just in time. I meet Ja Rule and my mates. We go straight into the studio and start work.

I've been here for more than two hours and we've just finished the track. Boy, I hope people like it, it's coming out in two months. Now I need a drink.

I'm going home now to get ready for *Party in the Park*. I'm wearing a great black top that I got in New York and some dirty denim jeans by Dolce & Gabana. They look beautiful! I'm having my hair put in ringlets by John Frieda. My make-up is wicked and I'm wearing tons of Cliniqué lip gloss, bronze eye shadow, tons of glitter, and I mean tons, and blusher.

Ha! The limo's arrived. I'm having a drink and some lunch. I'm *sooo* hungry. I'm getting close now. Boy, I'm starting to get butterflies in my stomach (maybe I should turn back?).

I'm here, there are *sooo* many people here, people are asking me for my autograph and my picture, it's so exciting. I'm an hour early, Atomic Kitten are on now. I've met Liberty X and Will Young, they're both really nice. Sandy and Spencer from Big Brother are standing over at the side.

Now I'm about to get on the stage. The crowd are going mad. I start with my new song, 'Foolish' and then sing my other ones. I'm absolutely loving it, the butterflies have all gone and I could stay up here all day but it's time for my last song, 'What's Love?' with Fat Joe. He is wicked. The crowd go even madder.

I'm off now but I have loved it *sooo* much on stage, I'm going to come next year. I still can't believe that crowd. It was amazing!

On my way home now, people are looking in my limo and waving and screaming.

At home, a quick change and out to a party.

3.30am. Time for bed, goodnight.

Sammy-Jo Greene (12)
Hampstead School, London

QUESTIONS

Why are we here? What happens when we die? Is there a reason?

These are all big questions. People have been asking them since there were people. When we don't understand something we create myths and legends around it. We keep on believing these even in the face of hard fact.

These questions are part of our existence. We always ask them but still we have no answers that we are prepared to accept. I have asked them, thought about them and considered them. Still I don't know the answers. No matter how far our knowledge grows, I doubt we will get an answer we will accept.

We want there to be more, we want a purpose, but why? That is what it all boils down to, what we all want to know. It is something we can never answer, for if we do then we will no longer have a purpose. The day we find it all out is the day we die.

Tom Wallace (14)
Hampstead School, London

A DAY IN THE LIFE OF AN ANT

This morning I woke up to the shrill noise of the danger whistle. I am a middle-aged ant (two months old) called Theo. I am part of a large colony and I am a soldier. My job is to protect our ant hill and by the sound of the loud whistle, I knew there was danger.

I climbed out of bed, through a hole in the wall and ran with the other soldiers into a tunnel. Our hill is made from a maze of tunnels that break into more and more passageways, like branches of a tree. We all know our way around like it's second nature.

We finally came to the main hall where we formed lines in alphabetical order. The chief soldier told us that an ice cream had been dropped onto the ant hill and was dripping in fast. The only thing to do was to dam it and make a channel for it go to down.

We were dismissed and we ran into the bright sunlight. The first thing we did was to gather twigs, mud and leaves to make a dam. When we had done this we started digging a channel. Once we were finished, the ice cream slowly started to run down the ditch like a white river.

Later on that day we all got a medal for bravery given by the queen ant followed by a royal banquet. Guess what we ate? *Ice cream!*

Carmen Bromfield Mason (11)
Hampstead School, London

A DAY IN THE LIFE OF A HONEYBEE

Today was a good day. It started off something like this . . . I collected heaps of pollen in an outstanding garden full of roses, bluebells, dandelions and many other flowers. It was all going well until I made my way into a house.

I made my way to every window and door there could possibly be. None were open. I buzzed around for ages and ages, trying to find my way out. I went back to where I came in from. It was shut. Then a human being was coming my way with a fly swat. I flew, but it was no use.

'Whack!' it went. The more I flew, the more aggressive the human whacked. I suddenly stopped. The human thought I was *dead*. I wasn't, I had lost a leg though. I was badly injured and it was getting dark. I tried to crawl, I couldn't. I tried to fly, it was hopeless. Maybe this was the end of my honey making life.

It was morning. I had been awake for ages and ages. A breeze came from a window- *a window!* I headed to it as fast as I could. I made it. *Freedom at last!*

I met a fellow honeybee outside. He told me how he'd been looking at me all night. He figured I'd been trapped in a house. I told him how a human tried to kill me even though I wasn't doing any harm.

We both went back to the hive, where all my friends greeted me. This was a life changing experience for me and one I'll never forget.

Zara Ahmed (12)
Hampstead School, London

A DAY IN THE LIFE OF WINSTON
(Written in the style of George Orwell)

It was a bright, crisp morning in August at about five minutes to nine. Winston Smith struggled up the road towards the massive white pyramid that was the Ministry of Truth. He was already sweating under the blue overalls of the party and his varicose ulcer had begun to itch in the growing heat.

As he entered the hot, crowded, noise-filled entrance hall of the 'Minitrue', he tried to hide his grimace from the numerous telescreens and the watchful eyes of Big Brother on the posters that covered the walls.

Once upstairs in his cubicle, Winston unrolled and clipped together three rolls that had arrived through the small pneumatic tube for written messages. Looking through them, he noted that they were all routine matters, though two of them would involve some tedious wading through figures. They read:

18.5.83 minipax malquoted success rectify
14.3.83 bb malreported eastasia rectify
3.2.83 miniplenty malquoted coffee rectify

He was summoned halfway through the first for the two minute Hate and then resumed his duties. The work took him through to lunchtime where he unsuccessfully tried to avoid his booming neighbour, Parsons, who was after some soap because of the recent shortage.

Having succeeded in securing the afternoon off, he walked home and had some Victory Gin before turning in for an early night.

Arun Sethi (16)
Hampstead School, London

THE START OF THE AUTOBIOGRAPHY OF ROB STERLING

When I was young I lived in a small village on the outskirts of Chester Le Street, Durham. It was a lively little place where everyone was happy and cheerful, apart from the odd few who were mainly drunks late at night.

In the village there was a Co-op for all your daily needs, also a newsagent run by a young lady called Bridget Cook and a post office. The most cheerful part of the village was a public house called The Olde England.

My family (the Sterlings) were a jolly old bunch. I can remember our Saturday night routine. It was a drink, some fish and chips and a board game, like Cluedo or snakes and ladders. Sometimes my best friend, George Smith, would come over with his parents, Joe and Jill.

George and I went to the school down the road, Lumley Comprehensive School. In the morning we would meet at my house and walk about ten minutes down the road to school. It was a good school in my eyes as it had a playing field the size of a football pitch.

My favourite teacher was called Mr Ratmon. He was an excellent scientist and could remember everything about the periodic table. He was short and stubby and walked a bit like a garden elf, but this did not stop me liking him. One day I had being playing football and was gasping for a drink, so he kindly gave me one.

James Wraight (12)
Langdon Secondary School, London

How The Centaur Came To Be

Once upon a time there was an old tramp who lived in London. This man was as dirty as possible. You couldn't blame him though; he had no money, one pair of clothes and was as skinny as a beanpole. He asked for little in life, only somewhere comfortable to rest, and for enough food.

One day the man waddled around, exploring London, when he stumbled across a dirty, over-used oven and beside it was a mouldy duvet. He didn't need to think twice about it, so hastily he wrapped the duvet around him and crept into the oven and was soon asleep.

Meanwhile, there was a horse that ran away from a zoo into an alley, as he needed the toilet. Wandering through the alley he came to a dirty, over-used oven. He peered inside. All he could see was a mouldy duvet. He looked to make sure nobody was looking and went to the toilet, in the oven. He was relieving himself when he tripped and fell into the oven and the door closed.

This was the oven that the man was in and, after hours of cooking, the door swung open and the man and the horse fell out. But, because they had been together for so long, they'd become welded to each other, with the duvet sticking them together, so there stood half man, half horse.

David Payne (13)
Langdon Secondary School, London

A DAY IN THE LIFE OF JONATHON TROYDON

Monday
Today I write this entry lying in the field hospital bed. I was told by Captain Reed to cover James Colt (field medic). Then I was told by Captain Reed, after covering James I was to go and fetch Steven Thompson (engineer).

After I got him he told me to cover him so he could blow a hole in the barbed wire, but I got a bit close and injured myself. The medic says I should be fine by late tomorrow.

I was lucky to be on the boat, as the boat next to us was blown to smithereens.

Tuesday
Nothing much to report but I heard 313 people died yesterday alone.

Wednesday
I completed my first mission today. I had to cross the minefield and get to the machine-gun. When I got to the gun there were five Nazis. I managed to kill them and completed the mission.

I have just been notified of our next mission. One hundred of our men are going in and we have reports that only 70-90 men are inside.

(Jonathon Troydon never returned).

Richard Everett (13)
Langdon Secondary School, London

SPIRIT

Hi, my name is Sue, I have been all alone since I was sixteen. When my mum and dad died they left the house and all the money they had in my name.

Since my parents died weird things have been going on in the house, what I mean by this is there is something like an evil spirit roaming about the house. You must be wondering how I know this. Well in the evening every day around seven or eight o'clock, while I am doing my homework, the lights turn off and so does the power in the house.

While the power is coming back on again the front door opens and then after a while I hear a sound go *boom!* that is the sound of the door being slammed. For a moment, while all of this is happening, I can feel a chill go up my spine.

On Sundays I go to pick up cherries from a nearby park, the cherries are kept in the part of the park where it looks like a forest, the trees are close together and while I'm walking I have the feeling I am being followed.

While I am picking the cherries the trees start howling and the way it starts swaying makes me feel like the tree is about to fall over.

I was walking down with my cherries when I found an eerie silence frightening, suddenly people had disappeared, gates were shut and there was no way out.

Dhivya Palliath (13)
Langdon Secondary School, London

THE FOOTBALL MATCH

Hi, I'm Stan and I'm a footballer in a county league. I've really got a story for you to hear and, if you're a person who likes football or even hates it, you're going to love my story.

It all started on a Sunday morning. It was a sunny day and our league team 'The Rovers' were practising in the park, as we do every Sunday, when we got a letter from the heads of the county league. It said that another team wanted to enter the league and, because we were the worst team in the league, they would replace us unless we could defeat them in a match on Monday at four o'clock.

Most people said they didn't mind but I told them to have faith in us. Sadly, as usual, the rest of the team didn't back me up, all they said was that this was probably a good thing, football was a waste of time, we never won, or even scored, football wasn't for us. I almost began to believe them.

Everyone then went home, but I stayed and practised. That night I had a dream. I dreamt that we were playing the match and won. I scored the goal, it hit me smack in the face and went in the goal. That was my greatest and only goal. I had scored.

In the morning, I bothered to show up to the match, then at least one of our players will have showed up I thought, but I was wrong. Everyone was there and the other team didn't show up, so we won.

So that's my story and it shows you, keep your enthusiasm and you just might make it.

Neil Kanhai (12)
Langdon Secondary School, London

THE INVISIBLE HOUSE

I was walking through the forest on a frosty, misty night when I saw a house. It looked very ancient and shabby. I decided to go inside the house so I knocked on the door, no one opened it so I went in.

It was very gloomy and dusty. The house was gigantic with a marble floor and a brown patterned ceiling. I saw a light on the other side of the room. It came closer and closer when I finally realised it was an old woman who was dusting. She didn't even notice I was there.

She had short grey hair, wrinkly skin and was wearing a black dress with a white apron on the top. She looked like a maid. Then she left and men in suits and women in puffy dresses arrived. They all started dancing together.

They were ghosts, I was so freaked out, they were dancing so peacefully together, I was shivering. It was like a dream. The dancers left the room and I was alone.

I started walking around when I touched a candle and my hand went right through it. Suddenly two men jumped out with swords and started fighting with each other. I ran to the door and kicked it open and ran out, when I looked back nothing was there at all.

Mahima Sundararaju (13)
Langdon Secondary School, London

GERMANY 0:BRAZIL 2

Ronaldo's two second half goals gave Brazil their fifth FIFA World Cup Championship and made sure they didn't do what they did against France in the World Cup '98 final. It was a hard fought and equally played match. But Ronaldo was on his day, which separated the two teams in Tokohama, Japan.

Ronaldo also lifted the golden shoe because he scored eight goals in the finals, three more than the next closed people who were Rivaldo and Miroslav Klose. Both countries played good football, which was entertaining to watch. Each team created a lot of chances; Brazil hit the woodwork near the end of half time. The first ever final between these two teams were entertaining and a dramatic end to the FIFA World Cup.

Germany came out looking very good in attack. Their first truly dangerous chance came when Schneider served a low cross from the right, which was for Klose, but the confused Brazilian defenders just about cleared it out for a corner kick (10 minutes had gone).

Germany continued to attack the Brazilian defence, and when Brazil seemed to be playing the worst they had done in the tournament, a wonderful through ball by Ronaldinho sent Ronaldo clear in front of the German goalkeeper Oliver Kahn. However, Ronaldo's cheeky shot with the outside of his left foot slide went well wide of the far post (19 minutes).

Ronaldo missed another chance minutes later. Again it started with a pass from Ronaldinho, this time a short chip over the top. Ronaldo's first touch pushed the ball too far forward, and Kahn was able to come off his line to come collect the ball from the Brazilian's weak toe poke (30 minutes).

With the half nearly ended, Brazil had a difficult chance. Kleberson, the Brazilian midfielder had a good look at goal on the counter attack, but his left foot shot rolled slowly wide of the right post (42 minutes).

Then it was Kleberson again going close, this time

with a shot from 25 metres that hit the crossbar (45 minutes). Then in stoppage time Roberto Carlos picked out Ronaldo at the penalty spot with a low cross, but Kahn made a spectacular save to deny Ronaldo (46+ minutes).

After going the entire first half without putting a shot on goal, Germany almost put one in the net two minutes into the second half. It came when a corner kick from the left found the head of Jeremies, but Edmilson saved the day for Brazil, stopping the powerful header with the help of his right foot (47 minutes).

Minutes later, Oliver Neuville gave Brazil a powerful free kick from 30 metres that Marcos stretched to get his hand on. He got a touch on the ball, which pushed it out for a corner (49 minutes).

With the famed Brazilians, Ronaldo, Rivaldo and Ronaldinho looking frustrated and Kahn looking unbeatable, suddenly there was some luck for the Brazilians. Ronaldo won the ball from Hamann in the German half and laid it off for Rivaldo, who fired a shot from 25 metres right at Kahn. Then Oliver Kahn fumbled the ball which wasn't hit hard, then the ball went right in front of the goal for Ronaldo, who slotted it into the net (0-1, 67 minutes).

Ronaldo needed no mistake from Kahn on the next chance. Kelberson started the chance with a run down the right side. He sent a pass into the middle that seemed for Rivaldo, but he dummied brilliantly, drawing a defender and letting the ball roll to Ronaldo, who shot perfectly from the edge of the area into the lower-right corner of the net (0-2, 79 minutes).

Oliver Bierhoff almost pulled one back for Germany with a powerful first time shot from 15 metres, but Brazil goalkeeper Marcos stretched well for the one-handed save (83 minutes).

And as time expired, Ronaldo could be seen shedding tears at the joy of his cup glory.

Anil Pillai (12)
Langdon Secondary School, London

A DAY IN THE LIFE OF A BABY-SITTER

I wake up at six o'clock every morning, get dressed and have my breakfast. This takes an hour. At seven o'clock I start my travels. I go on a train to Waterloo and walk down the road to my work.

I work at 59 Greenway Road. My job is a babysitter. It is really good fun because I love children. Anyway, I walk into the house and say, 'Hi,' then Miss Bruce, the children's mother, goes off to work and leaves me with the children. I make their breakfast and set out their toys. It's like a playgroup really.

I take them down the shops and buy some sweets. Then we walk back home and play for the afternoon. About one o'clock we have lunch.

After the kids have finished I clean them up and we play some more. They eat their snacks whilst playing with their toys. This is always a relief because it keeps them occupied. This allows me to clean up and start dinner, ready for when Miss Bruce comes home.

When Miss Bruce gets home it is time for me to go. So I walk to the train station, get the train down to London and catch a cab home. I make my own dinner, eat it and then fall asleep, all while sitting on the sofa watching television.

Lucy Graves (13)
Langdon Secondary School, London

BINKY BEAST

There once lived a beast, his name was Binky, he was a kind and gentle one too. He was as kind as a little old lady. But Binky was full of himself, he thought he was good looking. But also Binky lived in an enormous house, by himself. Except from his talking friends, which were a clock, candlestick and a teapot.

One day, outside a girl called Anna was taking her dog out for a walk, called Terrence when suddenly . . .
'Ouch,' screamed Anna.

Terrence had eaten one of her shoes. Anna was very cross and said to Terrence that she wouldn't buy him the wide screen TV for him to watch 101 Dalmatians.

She looked for a house nearby. She spotted one, it was Binky's house. *Bang!* went the door. Binky was surprised as he rarely had any visitors, he opened it.
'Hello, I'm Anna, I wondered if you had an old pair of shoes you could lend me?' asked Anna politely.

Binky saw that she had no shoe on her left foot. He looked at her and thought that she was tatty and ugly but felt sorry for her. He told her to come in. He got his mother's old shoe.
'Aichoo!' sneezed Anna.
'Bless you,' answered Binky.

He went to make her a hot chocolate. They both started talking and laughing, so was Terrence and candlestick. Inspite that she was tatty, Binky thought that she was a really nice person. So they became the best of friends.

Remember it's not the outside that counts, it's the inside.

Bhavini Chauhan (13)
Langdon Secondary School, London

MIDDLE EAST MESS

What is going on?

The Middle East is in a horrific state. George Bush wants the Palestinians to elect a new leader, but Tony Blair believes that the Palestinians should have the right to elect their own leader.

Yasser Arafat seems sure that Bush does not want him to stand down. Ariel Sharon has yet to comment.

The Palestinian people are baffled over the state of their country. Speaking to a Palestinian doctor made me realise, that the Palestinians just want peace.

They do not care about fighting over leaders. They just want an area of land to call their own, and to be able to live and work in serenity and unity.

This problem dates back to 1947. When Israel first came into existence, taking half of the Palestinian land. The people of Palestine have ever since been trying to claim back their land, and after three wars, have so far been unsuccessful.

The current issue is to find a way to have Palestinians and Israelis living side by side in peace. Both leaders of Palestine and Israel are being very stubborn. They refuse to trust each other.

George Bush and some other world leaders have asked the Palestinians to elect a new leader, who they can trust. Some world leaders seem to believe that Arafat has leanings towards terrorism. Will this problem ever be resolved?

Zakiyyah Ismail (13)
Langdon Secondary School, London

THE DAY I WAS A DOG!

Just last week I turned from a cat to a dog. It might sound unusual, and believe me it was, but I really wouldn't make a big deal of it. This is what happened.

As I woke on Monday morning I felt too big to fit in my cat basket so I got up and clambered out. As I rose I felt so heavy I nearly fell on the floor! I slowly heaved myself out and stretched out on the carpet. Then my owner came into the kitchen, I rose up waiting to be noticed.
She said, 'Where is that cat?' She looked at me and said, 'Ahh, what a cute doggy you are.'

Doggy! I had a good look at myself realising that I wasn't the cute tortoiseshell cat I used to be, I was a dog!

I had a sudden urge to lick my owner as she bent down to stroke my head, urgh! it was disgusting, I had foundation all over my tongue.

I slowly got used to my enormous weight, my slobbery mouth and my wet nose.

When I walked outside into the garden all the female dogs came walking towards me! Probably being a dog wasn't so bad after all! I mean I was never so attractive as a cat.

Apart from a dog's lack of hygiene, dribbling, over eating and excreting anywhere being a dog rocks!

Shreya Trivedi (13)
Langdon Secondary School, London

Roseabell

'It was a hot day when Lucy went out to play. Her mother had already gone to work and wouldn't be back till dinner time. So having the whole day ahead of her she decided to go exploring near the stream.

Lucy was just dipping her feet in the cold water when all of a sudden a small pink haired girl, with wings and a dress made out of rose petals appeared, hovering in front of her.

'Excuse me, I need your help, my name is Roseabell and I'm trying to escape from Zagnoll, the troll. He's my master and the only way to set me free is if he gives me a rose as a present. He's in your back garden, please help me!' the flower girl cried.

She then turned round and started to fly towards the little cottage. Lucy picked herself up and ran as fast as she could back home and through the garden where she saw a troll holding a flower. Lucy walked up to him and begged him to give her the flower.

'What's your name?' he asked.

'Roseabell,' Lucy answered.

'Sounds familiar, here you go, Roseabell,' the troll said, holding out his arm.

Then out of nowhere the fairy Roseabell grabbed the flower out of his hand and sent him home crying. Lucy and Roseabell then lived happily ever after.'

Rebecca shut her book and opened her desk enough to see a small pink haired girl with wings smiling back at her.

Ouma Hussain (13)
Langdon Secondary School, London

THE MAGIC SHELL

Long ago, in a small village, there lived a small girl called Rita. She longed to play with the children in her village but she had to help her mother work because they were not very rich.

One evening, Rita's brother David brought home some gifts from where he worked. David gave Rita a multicoloured shell and it looked very shiny and beautiful. Rita thanked him and she liked it very much.

When Rita woke up the next day, she found that there was a note attached to her shell.

It read, 'This shell will grant you three wishes, be careful what you wish for'. Rita was very excited with her new gift. She went downstairs to find her mother, her father and David eating some corn. Rita held her shell and closed her eyes. 'I wish my family were wealthy,' Rita wished.

She opened her eyes and instead of corn, her family were eating the finest foods, Rita was so happy.

After breakfast, David spoke to Rita. He said that she shouldn't be selfish with her wishes and he knew about the shell. In the afternoon, Rita was asked to help her mum. She refused to. Instead, she touched her shell and whispered. 'I wish I could play with all the children outside.'

Instantly, she found herself standing outside with the other children. Rita's mum was very upset, she went outside to call Rita back in.
'No!' Rita cried, 'I wish I could play outside forever.'

Rita felt herself whizzing, she had turned into a pigeon and flown away. She was never seen again.

Sally Nguyen (13)
Langdon Secondary School, London

WHAT THE MOON DID

As I ceaselessly crept through the menacing forest, the moon radiated its malignant scourge on me, I tried to avoid it, so it made no shadow. I tried to tread lightly and on, not on a stick or anything that made any sound. I tried to avoid bushes but if I wanted to stay safe I'd have to stay near the trees and the bushes in the shadows.

I could see an open field ahead of me. Should I chance it, or should I stay put? This thing, this satanic creature following me, why? What did I do to deserve this? *Crack!* A twig snapped underneath my foot. The sweat in my paws crept onto my face, the sweat on my forehead crept around my eyebrows, down the middle of my face and dripped off my nose. I slowly moved to wipe it off, as I did this I tried to make no noise. I knew any sound could blow my cover. Even though the macabre sky was a mysterious purple colour, it was still pitch-black.

I crouched down between two bushes and thought to stay here over night. My legs began to ache so I slowly moved closer towards the ground because I might as well get myself comfortable, as I was staying here all night and then when I wake or shall I say if I wake up I will make my escape . . .

Natasha Williams (13)
Langdon Secondary School, London

MYTH OF EARTH

The time will come when the planet of ice, also known as Pluto, will align with the fire star we know as the sun. The planet of electricity (Venus) will also align with the fire star. Once they perceive each other they shall be provoked to conflict and so there will be war.

A battle over each other's land will commence and all the misfires shall help bring the Earth closer and closer to destruction. From all this devastation and pain one shall rise with the hope of peace but shall fall with the feeling of war, thus the world shall be turned to ash.

All this can be stopped but only if the Chosen One successfully retrieves one element from each planet and the fire star and places them in a line and plays the melody of the Earth. Thus the norm shall be and peace be with all.

Niyi Ayorinde (13)
Langdon Secondary School, London

6 DAYS IN THE LIFE OF A CATERPILLAR - A DIARY

4 July 2003,   1pm
Dear diary
I've decided to write about my last few days as a caterpillar. I will continue later as I need to go and get some food.

3pm
Phew! That was a big lunch and what an appetite I have. Half a lettuce, a quarter of an apple, a quarter of a pear plus 4 leaves all in my stomach. Imagine that. Amazing or what. No wait, don't imagine that. It's too gross. Maybe it's because I'll become a . . . soon. I'm so glad you don't know. It'll be a huge surprise, believe me.

5 July 2003   5pm
I'm so happy; my friends are throwing me a party. Aren't I lucky? This is the first in ages. Well I suppose it's not often that a caterpillar becomes a . . .

6th July 2002   2pm
It's party time. I've just arrived and I'm so excited. I think I'm early because there's no one here. Well, I'll wait.

3pm
I've waited an hour and no one's here. I suppose I'd better go! Arrgghh! Sorry, everyone gave me a shock by surprising me. Well, I suppose I'd better go and get in the party mood. If you find spare time care to join me.

7th July 2003   Sunrise
I still haven't forgotten yesterday. The party finished just at 1am and I haven't slept a wink since! I can't remember the last time I had so much fun.

8th July 2003   Sunrise
I didn't sleep properly yesterday, I kept waking up dreaming of being a . . . only two days left till I'm a you-know-what. What you mean you don't know? Wait and see!

9th July 2003   1am
One day down and one to go. All my friends keep coming to see the new me (no, I haven't become a you-know-what yet), but they go a bit disappointed but partly pleased. I'm going to miss them.

10th July 2003   1pm
I've eaten 6 leaves, half an apple, half a pear and I'm sitting on a daisy. Why you ask, why? *How do I know!* Wait, let me see how beautiful I look today in the pond. I probably look like a fat slob. Oh my gosh! I'm a butterfly. I have to go find my friends and show off to them. Hey, I can *fly!*

Mariam Ramzan (13)
Plashet School, London

REBECCA PUMPKIN

As her reflection stared back at her, Rebecca Pumpkin looked at her weird figure in the mirror, wondering why people treated her differently at school. She was 13 years old, tall, thin and many people called her weird because she loved to wear dark colours, like black.

When she started school a student called Sarah Ann guided her round the school for 30 minutes. By 11am the tour of the school was finished and the bell rang for the lesson, which was English with a teacher called Miss Barnet. She introduced Rebecca to the class, then she showed her to her seat at the back of the class, in front of a troublesome boy who was trying to cut another girl's hair with scissors.

Rebecca sat in her seat and listened carefully to her teacher as she started the lesson with maths and then a girl across from her started talking to her called Rita Pond and was telling her how nice the school was and how kind the teachers were.

The lesson finished at 11.45 and it was time for break. As they walked out of the class someone burst out laughing behind them very loudly. They both turned round and saw it was the annoying boy.
'Oh my goodness,' Rita said. 'He cut a piece out from the back of your shirt.'
'Oh no,' Rebecca cried. 'Everyone thinks I'm weird now, I shouldn't have come here!' She then ran off crying until she reached her house. When she got there she ran straight past her parents and up into her bedroom where she began to write her diary . . .

Sade Thomas (13)
Plashet School, London

A STORY ABOUT A YOUNG GIRL

My parents don't know what to do with me. I'm kind of stuck but we will all be out of this mess in no time. I heard my mum and dad whisper to each other about what to do with me but I just sat there with my pet stroking him. Oh yeah, my parents had a divorce because they couldn't cope with each other anymore, especially when my mum used to start talking to my dad and they always started an argument. I didn't want to leave my house. I had a beautiful room which my dad had created himself.

We had a social worker at our house. She told me that I would be staying with Mum and the other week I would be staying with Dad. Now school was very far from the houses Mum and Dad were going to move into.

A few weeks later my mum and I moved in with Mum's boyfriend. He was as hairy as a baboon. He had two children, Zoë and Jordan, who were really annoying. The other week, when I went to visit Dad, he had moved out of his place, but we saw him on the way. He took me by car to his new apartment which was in the flats and in the basement. Dad had moved in with his girlfriend, Sarah, who had one daughter who was quite sweet, unlike Jordan and Zoë. Then I was going to Mum and Dad's place. It was all mad but I got used to it in the end and it was rather fun.

Komal Adrees (13)
Plashet School, London

THE LONELY FACE

We had moved to Beverley Road. Our new house was very dirty and had dust all over the place. We just had to clean it.

One day I was cleaning my bedroom and I saw a ladder leading up to a room where there was a face at the window. As I climbed it, it went to a dark and dusty room, but when I reached the window, the face had disappeared. The face that had been looking at me was a sad face. I wondered why. I really wanted to speak to the person, but I couldn't.

I waited for it all day, but it wouldn't come. I decided to go down to my room and wait there. After a while, I saw the face again, crying. I asked the face to wait for a minute and I asked, 'What has happened to you?' The face replied, 'It's a long story. when my parents died I had to stay with an aunt whom I hated very much. Once she tried to kill me but she couldn't. The next time she stabbed me with a knife and killed me. After that she left the house. Since then my soul has come out of my body. So day by day my body is disappearing. Now I'm only left with a face and I don't know how many days I will stay alive.'

Sana Abbasi (13)
Plashet School, London

AN ANSWER PLEASE

Dear Diary,

Today was an exciting day for me and kind of scary. A visitor came into our class to talk about religion. I got really mad and suddenly yelled in a loud voice, ' Why are there religions? From religion comes racism. God asks us to bring peace. With racism that can't happen. Religion brings racism to people. Every religion has proof of their beliefs, so why do we all have to believe in different things? Maybe when these proofs were left behind, the people who left them wanted to play with human nature. Nobody knows anything. Nobody knows what will happen after we die. You may think you do because of the evidence you happen to have, but others have evidence as well, so which religion is right? Meditation and enlightenment come into your life somehow, so why say it only comes from Buddhism, Christianity, Hinduism, Judaism and Sikhism? It should be in all religions. There is no proof from the past which says all the traditions and cultures we believe in are really existing materials.'

The teachers and children stared at me as I turned red. The visitor had no answer for me. She said she was getting late for another appointment and walked off. Just because she didn't give me an answer doesn't mean I won't find one. As my teacher always says, ' If you want an answer to a question which nobody gives you, try to find it yourself. Waiting for it to come never works!'

Samra Ahmad (14)
Plashet School, London

A DAY IN THE LIFE OF BLOODY MARY

I was born to King Henry VIII and Queen Catherine of Aragon on February 8th 1516. I was named Mary after my father's younger sister, Auntie Mary.

I was given the best tutors and studied the works of leading scholars. I could speak Latin, French, Spanish and could understand Italian but could not speak it.

When my father fell in love with Anne Boleyn, he came up with a very scheming plan. He planned to divorce my mother and used the text from the Old Testament, 'If a man shall take his brother's wife, it is an unclean thing . . . they shall remain childless.' Of course, he wanted a son to succeed to the throne when he died. He thought that God was sending a message telling him to divorce my mother in order to get a son.

Soon my father married Anne Boleyn and she gave birth to a baby daughter called Elizabeth. I was forced to hand the jewels over to the baby and I felt that I was not wanted because, at the time, I was in Richmond and was not allowed to see my mother. I was separated from my mother, confused and was torn between the two people I wanted to please most in life. My father even made me stop writing to my mother and I was not allowed to write one last letter to her. After all I had been through with my father's wives and his passion for a son, he died in January 1547. I was by his side when he died. I was finally crowned Queen in 1553.

Minakshi Rajput (13)
Plashet School, London

IT'S FAT LIFE

Fourteen-year-old Suzanne Thomas' belief that she could be loved if only she were thin, caused her nearly to go to the other world. Lying in Newham General Hospital, she said, 'I was so stupid, but then I didn't mind dying. Everyone was really horrible to me and teased me about my weight.'

She attended St Wannabies' where the reputation of bullying increased every second. Mr Johnson, head teacher of the threatening school said, 'It's a very sad thing that happened to Suzanne, but she must understand that she caused this herself. She can't blame the school for her selfish act!'
This proved what a lack of sympathy he had!

The Thomases were really devastated about what had happened to their daughter. Mr Thomas told us, 'It's because of me, and I'm really sorry, Suzanne. I should've listened to your problems and sent you to another school where you would've done well.'

He also told us that Suzanne was a very bright kid and had a brilliant sense of humour. 'I always told her that her weight did not matter and that kids need to grow.'
Another bright future has gone down the drain all because of the obsession of losing weight. The Newham Council representative said, 'As soon as Suzanne gets out of hospital, she will be starting Plashet Secondary School where the reputation of hard-working students has never ever failed.'

Let's just hope that this time the good-humoured girl gets what she deserves.

Nadifa Sheikhey (13)
Plashet School, London

SELF HARM

The air in the attic room was damp and humid. Moonlight poured in through the open window, filling the room with shimmering hints of midnight blue. The room was furnished with unwanted antiques. The girl sat on the window sill, lonely and still, cradling her knees to her chest, gazing far out at the brightly lit city. Besides her, lay several unused blades, the silver shimmering as it captured some of the moonlight. She looked down. How could she? How could she do it to herself, to the few people she cared about, day after day? Tears welled in her lifeless eyes as she thought back to the previous night. She sat on the same spot, in the same position, as she did every night and waited for her parents and the rest of the city to fall asleep, just so that she could be alone in a world full of people. As she did, she just sat there patiently, waiting, thinking. She thought and thought for many hours into the night about life, people, herself. She never seemed to find a way out no matter what she did. She felt trapped and alone, isolated in her own world. She did things, things she wasn't meant to do or which were seen as deviant.

She was depressed and knew she would make herself pay the consequences after the thoughts, that was after all, the most awaited moment. Why was she here? What was she worth? Why did others care what she did, or at least, pretend to?

She hated herself with so much venom that it made her shudder. She was dirty and sinful. No one noticed her, but that was what she wanted, to stay invisible to everyone so that they couldn't hurt her. She had a ways of making it work too. She'd just will herself to feel invisible with so much force that it worked. She sighed as she glanced at the blades. It was so tempting. The urge was so strong, but she would have to contain her temptation just for a while longer, till she was free. She fell into a deep trance once again and waited almost two excruciatingly painful, long hours.

The cool breeze swept her highlighted hair from her pale face. As it hit her face gently, she came into focus with a startled expression. *Yes,* she thought, it was time. She was so excited. It was as though her life would change dramatically.

She picked up the blade with a look of satisfaction on her face. slowly, competing with her urge, she punished herself. She brought the blades to her left wrist and pressed it in, slowly, so the pain would be greater as she slit her wrists. The pain was numbed, the blood spurted and drizzled down her palms. The process was so slow. She played with the blade on her arm. She couldn't care less if she slit open an artery or vein. She grinned, satisfied with herself. This was the life. The cuts burned, war and painful as her heart contracted. She cut in several places into the conceived arm she had permitted with blood. Deep red drizzled in all directions, the sight of the blood was almost heart-warming. The need to see the flow of the blood down her arms was so strong. As she pulled away hesitantly, she looked around her, she couldn't seem to be able to focus her eyes on anything. Tears brimmed in her eyes, and as one lengthy streak rolled down, she gave way and collapsed onto the ancient wooden floorboards.

Rubina Khalique (15)
Plashet School, London

THE LIFE OF A TUDOR WOMAN

I was taught from birth that I was inferior to men. I was told that all women were said to be the only imperfection in God's creation.

I was given hardly any personal freedom. I was raised to obey my parents. I was also taught that my only function in life was to marry and bear children. I was taught to be obedient to my husband and I have to learn in silence from him.

My parents did not believe in education for me, nor did anyone else's parents. No one thought that education was good for girls because they thought that they would spend most of their time and skills on writing love letters. Most girls at young age were taught the wifely arts. Their fathers, like mine, mostly chose husbands of upper class girls for them. Very few women and men of noble birth chose their own partners. Marriage was often held for political reasons. The idea of marrying for love was considered bizarre and foolish. My marriage happened as I never saw my husband until my wedding day. This often happened. My marriage took place when I was 14. A girl's chance of getting married depended more on her wealth and the social position that her family were in than her beauty and accomplishments.

Men expected to rule their wives and thereby gain their love. Sex before marriage was forbidden. I was taught that sex was only for the breeding of children, so the word of God can be passed through.

Nagajothi Ravichandran (13)
Plashet School, London

DIARY OF MOTHER TERESA

I was born on 27th August 1910 in Shkup (Skopje.) My mother's name was Nikolle and my father's name was Dranafille Bojaxhiu.

I decided to devote my life to God when my good friend and I, Lorenc Anotoni (who was known as a composer), were returning home from the Catholic Church in Letnica, in Vitia, Kosova.

After the age of 18 I joined the Irish Catholic Order of the Sisters of Loreto. After spending sometime in Ireland, I went to Calcutta, where I taught geography, history and catechism at St Mary's High School. Then later I became the principal of the school, and mastered Hindi and Bengali.

In 1930 I was given the name Teresa, in honour of St Teresa of Avila, a Spanish saint of the 16th century.

I left St Mary's High School and began working in the slums of Calcutta among the poor. In 1950 I found my order, the Missionaries of Charity, whose work, as I defined it, was to provide 'free service to poor and the unwanted, irrespective of caste, creed, nationality or race.'

In 1952 I established a home for the dying destitute and soon after I opened my first orphanage.

Over the years I had used the money obtained from such awards to set up mobile health clinics, homes for alcoholics and drug addicts, and shelters for homeless.

In 1980 I visited Kosova. Eight of my charity houses operate in Albania and two in Kosova. The largest charity organisation in Kosova carries my name.

I was hospitalised several times in 1996 with heart, lung, kidney and other problems.

Sabita Suppiah (13)
Plashet School, London

TRIBULATION

High up in their stormy castle, the royal couple waited for the birth of their first child. It had to be a boy; a girl would be bad luck for their name. The Devil demanded a boy child; it would be death to disobey him. Alivia whispered her final prayer:

> 'Bring us a boy
> Don't do me wrong
> Or all your joy will be gone, gone, gone.
> Vanished
> Banished
> Your enemy's gone
> You're the evil if you bring the wrong.'

Midnight: witching hour. A scream pierces the night. 'No!' A new life has been created. A female life! The curse was unleashed.

As the child was taken from her, Alivia wept and wept. She dragged herself from her bed and staggered towards the nursery. There, lying beside the crib, was her dead husband, Amezi. There was commotion all around her as servants rushed about in panic. Numb with grief, Alivia picked up her newborn baby and quietly slipped out of the castle towards the lake.

Kneeling at the water's edge, Alivia parted the rushes and gently laid her daughter in a tiny basked hidden there. 'Hera, Hera is what your father would have called you,' she said. The baby gazed back, red-eyed. There was a faint smile on her lips.

Alivia walked out into the cold water of the bottomless, frozen lake. The only sound was a distant laugh carried on the wind.

Kristina Smith (13)
Swadelands School, Kent

MARIA'S LIFE

Maria could not run any further. She had to stop. She fell to her knees, trying desperately to catch her breath for she knew she was running late. She had bags under her eyes, since she had been up all night washing her clothes. It was now 6am, time to go back to work.

Maria, her mother, three sisters and two brothers lived in a tiny house in the countryside, away from the village. She was on her daily trip to the shop in Little Brand, which is the nearest within a mile.

All of Maria's brothers and sisters went to school while she was left to clean the house. She did this while her drunken mum lay in bed smoking and drinking.

Maria didn't have any friends, and none of the villagers spoke to her because they disagreed with Maria's mother. If she didn't finish her evening jobs, her mother made her sleep outside, even in the freezing winter. Maria had a back-breaking, tiring life, working non-stop, with no thanks but a beating. Even her brothers beat her for no reason.

When Maria was seven, people started to get angry with her mother for making Maria do such things. The villagers decided to do something about it, so they called the police who took Maria's mother away. Maria was pleased but her brothers and sister were upset because their mum was nice to them. They got through okay, the oldest sister looked after the younger children and everyone helped out in the house. Maria went to school and, although she was behind, she soon caught up.

At last Maria had a happy life, but her past would never be forgotten.

Laura Dartnell (13)
Swadelands School, Kent

SKATE ON BOY

In the year two thousand, a lad named George and his friends Edward, Jamie and Henry were in the skatepark. All his friends dared him to jump off 'the killer' on his skates. Nobody had ever jumped off 'the killer' on skates. He took the dare.

He started to skate. He was going fast. He looked up at the jump again. Sweat was running down his face and the crowd was roaring. What a jump it was! He looked up proudly, but was he ever going to do it again? You could see he was scared. He started to skate towards the jump-offs. He was off. His nan quickly called the ambulance.

He went into hospital and they spoke as if George was very lucky. He had a broken leg and arm. It was a lucky escape, but his nan didn't think it would be this serious.

His friend got arrested but George didn't because he was in hospital and couldn't have done anything wrong. The police asked a few questions but they believed him because he seemed as if he was being honest.

A few days later, he was better but his nan had died. He was left everything, including loads of money. He was able to go to school and he never got on a pair of skates again.

Richard Down (13)
Swadelands School, Kent

WORLD CUP FOOTBALL

It was a warm day in France 1998. It was June 1st, World Cup day. England played against Germany and won 5-1. Celebrations went on in a pub nearby. At about midnight, people came out of the pub and saw German fans. The German fans started throwing stones at us. Neil (my friend) couldn't take it anymore. He got a bench and threw it at them. They were knocked down. Then all the English and German fans charged at each other and started fighting. A couple of them pulled out knives and stabbed each other. Moments later, French police came down with riot shields. The police thought they should call for back-up and did. Ten minutes later, a squeaky noise was heard.

Some of the people stopped and looked around. They saw a laser cannon and Neil shouted, 'There's a water cannon'
So everyone broke the windows in McDonald's, got chairs and ran back outside. When they got out, the police sergeant shouted, 'Fire!'
So they turned on the water cannon and lots of fans went flying. Some stood their ground and tried to fight. Some ran and escaped.

They kept on fighting but eventually they all collapsed and the police came down, grabbed some people and put them in a cell nearby. Five hours passed and the people in the cell were released, all except Neil. He had to go to hospital because someone had cut his skin and he had to have twenty stitches.

Jamie Kriehn (12)
Swadelands School, Kent

MY BEST FRIEND

I woke up in a sweat again last night, this was the third night in a row. It's a year tomorrow when it happened.

I became lonely, my dad died. He was like my only friend, not just my dad. We would go swimming every day together and did things that normal father and sons didn't do.

Today, I got my first invitation. It was from Jonny Depth, he was my age. I'd only met him a couple of weeks ago, that's why I was so surprised when it arrived. Dad said I could go, but was a bit worried because he had heard rumours going around about his party.

The day of the party finally arrived. I got ready about 8.30pm. We got in the car and left, and before you knew it, he was off on his little lecture. All he kept on about was drugs and drinking. I yelled out, 'Stop treating me like I'm a little kid. I'm 11 years old. We're too young for all that stuff!'
He turned and looked at me. It was like a look of disappointment. He had taken his eyes off the road for one second. That's when it happened. A dog ran into the road, I yelled out, 'Watch out!'
My dad swerved and smashed into a tree. I was knocked out for a couple of minutes. Then all I remember was waking up and smelling gas, so I finally got myself together and managed to climb out of the car and get round to my dad's side. I couldn't seem to move him, so I decided to go for help.

There were a lot of cars going past, but none seemed to stop, but finally one car stopped. There was a young lady inside. I told her what had happened and she quickly pulled out of her bag her mobile phone and dialled 999.

A short while after, the police and paramedics arrived. They soon got to work. The police shut off the area, whilst one paramedic checked me over and the other one checked my dad. That's when I thought he was going to be all right, because the paramedic didn't need anyone else's help, but boy, was I wrong.

All of a sudden, he started shouting all these things like, 'Get the crash set quick,' and 'Now!' I was so scared when they were shouting, and all

those beeps, then it stopped. I shouted, 'No, you've got to keep trying!' then I burst out crying. One of the paramedics came over and asked, 'Are you alright?'
I turned round and said, 'What do you think?'

My mum, Sue and brother John turned up. My mum knew straight away what had happened.

So, there you go. That's when I became lonely, plus I lost my best friend, my dad.

Jodie Slade (12)
Swadelands School, Kent

THE HAUNTED YARD

It was the 14th November 1992. It was a cold, wet and windy day. A farmer called Barry Kent had just died, but no one knew how. The police think he had had a heart attack. He was 82 years old. He had a grey and black hat that he always used to wear. He wrote a will when he was 32 years old, which said that he wanted to be buried in the field that he kept his sheep in.

Two years later; two girls, one called Sophie, who was nine years old, and Jade, she was seven years old. They are sisters and they went to the field to play football. Jade kicked the ball far away, so Sophie ran after it.

About five minutes later, Sophie shouted, 'Jade, come over here!'
Sophie ran to Jade, feeling very scared. 'What's wrong?' she asked.
'I heard a scream,' Sophie replied.
'Don't worry, it was probably someone playing around,' Jade said.
They both walked back, feeling very scared.

Suddenly, they stopped. 'What's that?' Jade enquired.
'It looks like a grave,' Sophie replied, feeling like she was just about to scream.
'But, who would want to be buried here?'
'I don't know. Let's go and tell Mum and Dad,' Sophie begged.

They ran home and they told their mum and dad. Then they all went up to the field. Sophie and Jade both showed them the grave. They all walked back in silence.

When they got back, they all sat down and their mum said, 'That's Barry Kent's grave and old farm.' She started crying.
'Barry Kent was your mum's friend. I don't want you ever going there again, okay?' their dad said.
'Okay,' they both replied.

They never went there again.

Jenny Wicks (12)
Swadelands School, Kent

THEIR BEACH

I wondered why my hair never grew. My knees had no scratches. I also wondered why I didn't get any taller.

Down by the sea, me and my four sisters ran and played noisily without a care in the world. Until a day, not long before Easter, at the sea's edge.

'Oh do catch up, Carrie,' Mary shouted to me from afar.
'Coming,' I squeaked. I had taken an interest in a shell I could see and wandered over.

Clouds came over, light vanished from the sky, a light, eerie figure appeared, which looked like a small, elderly lady. She looked cold and pale like a ghost. The four of us screeched, my sisters had seen it too.

As the heavens roared and hailstones fell, we ran, gliding across the sand.
'Don't be silly girls,' my gran protested, when we scrambled into the cabin. The rain crashed noisily on the wooden roof.

The next day, Gran walked to the bright, yellow beach with us, when the sand turned grey and the same dark clouds appeared. Gran could see the figures too, and whispered nervously, 'I know who they are.' With a shrill voice, 'I can see them clearly.' Then she shouted, in a panicked rage, 'They're spiritualists!'

So you can see, back then, on that day I found out, that what we saw were not the ghosts.

We were!

Rebecca Lewington (13)
Swadelands School, Kent

THE DEVASTATION WAITING TO HAPPEN

I remember it was during the summer of 1991 that it happened. Me, Roger and a few other men were asked to take a cargo load of oil to America, which meant we would have to travel across many seas. That night, before I went to bed, I started packing all the things I would need for the trip to America. Even though it would soon be floating around somewhere or even at the bottom of the ocean.

As I rubbed the sleep from my eyes, I could see the sun blazing through the curtains, onto my face. I realised I had overslept, so I jumped into my clothes that I'd laid there the previous night, grabbed my suitcase and stopped at the bakers, on the way to the dockyard, to get a cheese and onion roll.

As I entered the road to the dockyard, I could smell oil and a kind of musty smell. As I got closer, the smell was getting stronger and stronger, when I got out of the car, I could hear the captain calling the register out and everyone answered to the captain, whether they were all present or not.

After the captain had gone through the register, all the rules and where we had to go, we climbed onto the ship like a stampede of elephants. We were all shown to our rooms, sorted out our luggage, and had to go to the main eating area where we would soon be having many meals, the captain gave us our uniform and we got on with our jobs.

A week later, we had arrived at America and we were allowed to have the weekend there, but as it happened, we had to leave early because of storms. So we climbed back on board the ship, like we all did the day we first arrived at the dockyard. The captain called out the men's names again and everyone was present.

We were halfway through the week, I was getting ready for bed because I only worked days. All through the night I could hear the waves crashing against the side of the ship, it was about 3 o'clock in the morning and I decided to get up for a glass of water. Roger was still snoring in the bunk above me. I managed to climb over all the mess which was on the floor, get a cup of water and get back in bed.

Suddenly, *thud!* My head whacked against the wall. I looked out of the window and all I could see was like a black blanket spread across the night sky!

As I woke up Roger, we both rushed out into the corridor, there was silence, then a great gush of water filled the corridor. All our stuff was everywhere and that's when I lost Roger. I rushed one way and he must have gone the other way.

The ship was sinking and that's when we had to make a decision. Do we jump now or wait? Then I remembered the little boat. I managed to cut the rope. Lots of men jumped in, far too many.

As we got away from the ship, I realised Roger was still on it, but there was nothing we could do apart from sit and watch!

Soon after the ship was nearly sunk. It felt like my heart was going to stop beating. There was oil all over the sea and there was a rescue boat coming our way and we managed to attract its attention. They took us to hospital and no one was hurt. Here are the names of the people who never made it: Luke, Roger, Ian, Peter, the captain, Andy and Matthew.

This was the devastation of the summer of 1991.

Kerry Stevens (13)
Swadelands School, Kent

THINGS HAPPEN FOR THE BEST?

I'm not your average, everyday girl. I'm 13 and quite tall for my age. I've also got one younger brother, Dane. You're probably thinking, well, what's not so average about that? So here goes. When I was only a few years old and Dane was a baby, our mum died and Dad couldn't cope, so we got sent here. Yeah! Great!

In total there are about 30 of us and we all get along fine. It's as if we're all brothers and sisters. We all live in this huge house, by the sea, with the grouchiest carers, ever!

There are some pros to living here though, all my friends live here as well, so we have a right laugh. We have talent contests, karaoke nights, make up dances, do each other's hair and make-up and play pranks.

Well, this is what we did do, until my brother and I got adopted by this really nice couple, Mr and Mrs Branezon and their 17-year-old son, Danny. (I've always wanted an older brother!)

They went sailing one day and got more than they bargained for when they came here. (There was a storm and their boat got caught in a wave, they then sailed to shore and came here.)

They, (the Branezon family) got back on the plane to England, but with two extra people. Me, Sara, and my brother Dane! We've always wanted to be adopted, but, don't get me wrong, they are brilliant people, but I just want to live in the care home with my friends! Wouldn't you?

Kaylie Cairns (13)
Swadelands School, Kent

THE LIGHTHOUSE FAMILY

It all started 10 years ago. We, the Smiths, decided to get away for a week on an island in the sea. It was an odd place to go, nice and quiet. My wife Sue, 32, and two children, Paul, 13 and Lucy, 10, were very tired and ready to go home the next day, until something terrible happened.

We were all getting ready to get on the boat and go home. We all got on the boat and were about to leave, when Lucy told us she had forgotten her Frisbee. She climbed back up the rocks to get it, and suddenly, her foot slipped and she fell into the freezing cold water. I looked down into the water, but I couldn't see her anywhere. Then I saw a splash, and jumped in to save her. It took about three minutes to get her out of the water, but I was as quick as possible. She wasn't breathing, so we kept trying until we got to the shore.

When we got there, we called for an ambulance and they rushed Lucy to hospital. After about an hour of waiting, the doctor came out and said she didn't have much of a chance. Eventually she died. We were so upset about the accident, that we moved onto the island, and for money, worked in the lighthouse. It's hard to cope with the death of Lucy, but we are managing here on the island.

Roxanne Day (12)
Swadelands School, Kent

THE FIRE STARTER

It all began in the 1990s, when Bob travelled back in time to the 1980s. He went in a time machine to America. It all ended up in a big disaster and Bob never returned, because of his jealous brother, Joe.

When Bob eventually got to the 1980s, he went and stayed in an hotel called 'The Royal Star', meanwhile, a man called Joe knew about this and he knew who he was because Bob was his rich twin brother!

Joe went and started a fire at The Royal Star Hotel because if he killed his brother, he would get all of his money. The fire got worse, the flames spread all over the building and Bob couldn't get out. Then he collapsed, but luckily for Bob, some firemen came and got him out of the building. He got rushed to hospital for special care.

Eventually Joe got caught by the police and was put in jail. Sadly, Bob didn't make it through the night. Joe said he didn't mean to kill Bob, but did he?

Joe felt really bad about going to jail, so he changed into a nicer person than he was. He ended up serving an eight year sentence in prison. He deserved that!

Christopher Barrett (12)
Swadelands School, Kent

THE LONDON JOB

It was 1994 when it happened. My daughters got killed doing a job for me. £10,000 for dropping some drugs off to Konche, the hardest man going. It all went well until the packet of drugs fell out. Then it all went downhill.

It was the morning of the job. The girls went through the routine once more and went to do the job. That was the last time I saw them. I had a phone call at 2.30pm saying they had dropped the drugs off. At 3.30pm, I had a phone call saying there was a bomb in the car. The money was going up with them. The Chinese gang were chasing them. Before they said anything else, there was a loud bang. I got my gun and set off to find the Chinese gang. I saw them, 'round the car, trying to find any money.

As I drove past, I shot them all in the head. I did not look for any money, I just got the remains of my daughters. The next day, I buried them in my garden.

That was two years ago. I'm now remarried and have two boys. Not all things turn out as bad as you think.

Luke Goody (12)
Swadelands School, Kent

ANNABEL, BE STRONG

In the summer of 1941, down a quiet street, lived a young mother, Heather and her lovely six-year-old daughter, Annabel. Heather knew the bombs would soon hit their house, so she started packing clothes and food in a small bag. Annabel didn't really understand what was going on, so she started packing her favourite toys in a small carrier bag.
'No, Annabel. We can't carry anything we don't need,' Heather said.
'Oh!' moaned Annabel.

Then a doodlebug bomb flew over and dropped in their garden. Part of the bedroom roof collapsed on Heather!
'Mummy, Mummy talk to me! Mummy?' the single tear turned into a thousand.

Soon, other parts of the house started falling. Annabel thought for a moment, Mummy always told me that if a bomb was to fall, I should run and take a gas mask.

As Annabel ran, she tried to picture what life had been like, when her mummy would buy her sweeties every Friday.

By the time night fell, Annabel was cold, scared and hungry! Then a voice was heard. It was an old lady. She whispered to Annabel, 'Hello dear, my name is Bell. You can come with me, if you want?'
She pushed out her hand. Annabel touched Bell's hand. They quickly walked down the path to a posh looking house. Annabel remembered that tomorrow was the day when Mummy was supposed to be sending her to the countryside to be safe. 'Tomorrow, am I going to the countryside?' Annabel questioned.
'No, you will stay here because you're a bad girl. Now wash my clothes!' Bell's attitude soon changed . . .

Three years later, and today was Annabel's ninth birthday. All she got was a good beating and no food! It had been like this since that sad night when they met. If Annabel were to run away, she would have nowhere to go.

Soon, at her school, the teachers noticed the belt marks on her legs. That night, the police and social services came round and arrested Bell. From that night, Annabel stayed in a children's home until she was 16 years old.

When Annabel reached her twenties, she trained to be a nurse.

Emma Gasson (13)
Swadelands School, Kent

FOOTBALL CRISIS

Jemma was playing footie with her friend Jodi, when she kicked the ball too hard and it landed on Jodi's face. She fell to the ground. Jemma called her mum, Ally. When Jodi came round, Ally decided to take her to A&E.

When they arrived, the doctors took Jodi into a cubicle while Ally phoned Jodi's mum, Hannah. While Jemma was waiting for Jodi to recover, she spotted two nurses playing cards so seriously, so she went over to them. 'Hello, why are you playing here?' Jemma asked.
'We're practising for the world card's championships,' one of the nurses said, with a cool look on her face.

Meanwhile, one of the doctors had come to give them some news. 'Jodi has concussion, but she may not be able to remember some of your names, but after the concussion wears off, she'll be able to remember everything except the accident, which may frighten her, so please be careful. You may go in and see her now.'
'Thanks.'

But as they walked in Jodi screamed, jumped up out of the bed and ran, out of a window and out of the car park onto the main road and to the right.

Meanwhile, Ally was trying to calm Hannah down. 'Do you have any idea where she'd have gone if she was scared?'
'Her treehouse, it's at her nan's house.'
They rushed to Jodi's nan's house, she was there. Jodi calmed down two days later.

Jemma Cresswell (13)
Swadelands School, Kent

THE HORRENDOUS FIRE AT WATERLOO

The story is set in Waterloo, London, on the 25 December 1989.

Sam Ballden is a 12-year-old boy who didn't have many friends. He had dark hair with light blue eyes. When he got home he went shopping in Waterloo, he walked into a computer game's shop and he found the game which he'd always wanted. He took it out to the back of the shop to put the disk in the case.

Whilst he was waiting, two tramps set fire to the shop. They didn't know what was happening, when they walked through the shop, Sam saw the roaring flames. He didn't know what to do but he telephoned the Fire Services to come to the scene.

Eventually when the firefighters arrived, the fire had already spread to the next shop. A fireman came into the shop and rescued Sam and the shopkeeper from the roaring flames. When they were out of the fire, they were passed straight to the paramedics. The fire was on the news and it lasted three days - Sam escaped with minor burns to the hands and face.

The shop re-opened three months later. Sam will never forget the experience of being in that fire. He was given some free games from the shopkeeper for staying calm and being brave in the fire.

Matthew Shrimpton (12)
Swadelands School, Kent

THE UNUSUAL DAY

Once upon a time, there was a family. Mum (Hannah), Dad (Andy), a brother (Dan) and two sisters (Louise and Samantha).

The Mum asked the 11-year-old sister to go and get some milk, so Louise started to walk down the road to the shops. All of a sudden, Louise stopped and stared at the sky . . . there was a flash and a smash, the milkbottles had fallen out of Louise's hands, and she disappeared into thin air. All of a sudden, she was in a spaceship.

'Where am I? she screamed. She heard no one reply to her call. 'Hello, is anyone home?'
'Someone is home.'
'Yes, who?'
'Aliens, of course.'
'Let me see you.'
'Yes, as long as you don't scream.'
'I promise.'

So they came out and they were hideous.
'Told you I wouldn't scream. Why do you want me here?'
'We need your help.'
'My help? Why me? You could have gone for anyone in this town.'
'We know that, but you're rich.'
'What has that got to do with me?'
'Well . . .'
'Well what?'
'Well, we think because you're rich, you have a magic power that can get rid of the aliens that have taken over our planet.'
'I haven't got any magic powers. I have only got two pints of milk. Hey, where are my milkbottles?'
'Oh, here they are, you dropped them when we picked you up from Earth.'
'So, if I help you, you'll let me go, but if I don't help you, you'll keep me here?'
'Yes.'

Louise thought to herself, I know what I could try. I could put milk on them, that might kill them.

When Louise got out of the spaceship, she tripped over the step, and spilt some milk over the aliens. They all fell down, shrivelled and disappeared.

'Now I can go home!' Louise cried.

She went home and never forgot that day.

Toyah Gray (13)
Swadelands School, Kent

ALL ABOUT MONEY!

In the glorious years of the sixties, at Greenich Secondary school, exams were coming up. Harry hadn't revised for them and was mega worried, especially maths, science, English and geography! He was so worried he was getting stressed, with himself, and with his family, and friends.

Then, he met a stranger on the streets. He was a rough looking boy, about the age of 13 - scruffy, with dark hair, brown eyes and very yellow and black teeth.
'You look stressed, my dear friend.'
'Tell me about it. I mean, have you seen how much I have to revise for tomorrow? Stress isn't the word for it! Anyway, I'll see you around,' said Harry.
'Wait a minute, young friend, I might have something for your little stress problem in this pocket of mine,' said Rupert, cunningly.
Out came some white stuff, in a money bag, which looked like chalk, but Harry knew it was drugs.
'That will be £20 please!' demanded Rupert.
'I haven't got that much money! I'll bring it tomorrow, I promise,' said Harry.
'Very well. *Tomorrow!*'

The next day was a Tuesday and Harry was feeling a lot better. He knew full well that drugs could damage his health and he was putting his life in danger. He was a bit stressed though! About money! He'd forgotten the money for Rupert. He was going to be hurt for sure. He knew by the look on Rupert's face, when he walked down the gravelly path.
'You haven't got my money, have you! I can tell you haven't by the look on your face,' shouted Rupert.

Harry ran for his life to Professor Magonagol and hid under her cloak. She grabbed Rupert by the neck and locked him in a cupboard.

Rupert died of dehydration and starvation the next day. This is what you get for being greedy with money. Harry had learnt his lesson.

Charley Ashby (12)
Swadelands School, Kent

THE BOMBING

Ice. Nothing but ice. An old man, tall and wrinkly, drove his way to a new investment, a shop. He drove very carefully through the thick, slippery ice. He had been on the road for two hours and he could see the shop a mile away, as he was in the middle of nowhere. As frost dropped from the tree branches, he could see a plane, a B17 bomber, circling around the old man's shop.

The old man wanted a photo of him standing outside his house, to put in the shop window. He lined up his camera and put it on the timer. He ran and stood proudly. When the flash went, he could hear a small screech, like a mouse, then *boom!* A bomb had hit his house with a tremendous bang. He got chucked up in the air and him, and the camera, were buried for 60 years.

The present day.

'Pictures. We need pictures,' the news editor shouted. 'This mystery crater is a goldmine. If we get a good angle on this, we could make millions,' he repeated.

At the same time an explorer called Sir Mark Davies, was appointed head explorer of the crater. Mark called his crew, Ashley, Sam, Chubby and Jack, roughly the same build and size. He was the joker of the group.

As they set off, they took the same road as the old man, all frosty and creepy. When they reached the crater, there was a foul stench. As Mark jumped in the crater, the ground shook, then Jack, Ashley and Sam followed. They had found a huge lump of rock.

Once they had dug it out they could see it was a comet. They, at last, had a theory. Yes, a comet.

Once they had come to remove the comet, they revealed a shop, all crushed and burnt, and an old man, rotting. Once they had removed the shop and the body, they uncovered a bombshell and a camera.

Once they had got the camera, they developed the picture and released it to the press, so they had a story. But how did the comet get there? I guess we will never know.

Mark Davies (13)
Swadelands School, Kent

THE BIG ZILLA

One day on an island full of lizards and insects, a scientist found some eggs and they didn't know where the eggs came from. Later that day, the eggs hatched out and a big lizard came out of the egg . . .

Three years later the lizard was as big as the Twin Towers, he went to New York but no one knew . . . yet!

Big Zilla laid loads of eggs under New York. The people were suspicious because sometimes New York would shake.

The next day Big Zilla came up and the whole of New York stayed in their homes. The army was called in to try to destroy the monster, they tried everything to destroy it, but they couldn't because it was too big and strong. The army tried to use some very big weapons against him. One night they tried to destroy him with bait, they used fish to get the monster where they wanted. After an hour, the monster came up and after a countdown, loads of guns were firing, but the monster ran away.

The next plan was to chase the monster to a bridge and get him tangled in wires. Big Zilla was on the run and after 30 minutes he got caught up and died from all the shots fired at him.

Aaron White (12)
Swadelands School, Kent

TOMLIN DRAGON

Tomlin got up, he looked around, he was situated in the middle of a deep, green forest on a long, stone pathway. He looked down, picked up his rucksack and threw it on his shoulders. Tomlin set off on his journey.

It wasn't long before he spotted a small paper object in the lush, green grass. He bent down and picked it up. It was a tatty, old, yellow map and on it was what seemed to be a map of the deep forest. Tomlin looked at the map of the deep forest and found that he was on the temple path which lead to a large scaled building, named the Temple of Doom. Tomlin folded up the map and placed it deep into the bottom of his pocket. He set off back and estimated his journey to the temple of Doom to be half an hour.

He arrived at the temple, there were small stones crumbling off the side of the building. He saw an opening straight in front of him, he could only see darkness beyond the temple's entrance, then he plucked up his courage and dived in. He stumbled through the doorway and looked around. 'Oh my god!' gasped Tomlin. There was thick mould dribbling down the dirty, cracked walls. Tomlin looked forward and there was a door left slightly ajar and behind it all Tomlin could see was a bright, white light. But what could it be? thought Tomlin.

Alex Rush (13)
Swadelands School, Kent

HOW I BEAT UP THE BULLY

There once was a boy called Frank Smith. It all started when I kicked my football at him and he just stared at me. After school I went through the park and as I was coming to the end, he came through the gate. He got me by the neck and pushed me against the wall and he beat me up. At the end, he flicked my glasses off my face and stamped on them. Then he ran off.

I was so angry, I chucked a stone at him and it hit him on the back, then I ran all the way home. When I got home no one was in, I ran upstairs and washed, then got my spare pair of glasses and put them on.

I rang up my uncle, he was the only one I could trust not to say anything. I told him what he had done to me and he said that he would teach me how to box.

A year passed, every day after school the bully would beat me up and every night my uncle would teach me boxing. It was Friday the 13th of October, after school I went through the park. For the first time, he was waiting for me, he walked up to me and he swung at me. I moved and he hit the wall, he looked very angry he turned around. I took my chance and punched him in the face. Then I hit him in the stomach and he fell over on the floor crying. I looked at him and told him that's how I've felt, every day.

I ran home and I told my uncle. The bully never touched me again.

James Plummer (13)
Swadelands School, Kent

WIN SOME, LOSE SOME

Do you ever feel that something which happened years ago seems it was just five minutes ago? You're probably wondering what I'm talking about!

The year was 1995 and the day was Thursday, the month was April. It was the day when I lost everything I owned, but gained something as well. Does that sound like a riddle? Well, let me explain.

On the night of the fire, my family were sitting down for a meal. We've recently had a new addition to our family, my little brother Johnny. We were all discussing what to do at the weekend when my mum thought she could smell petrol. 'Can you smell that?' Mum asked. I sniffed. A stench ran up through nose, Mum and Dad went to check it out.

I waited and waited, the dinner turned stone-cold, nobody came. The smell started to get so strong that I decided that I would take Johnny and go outside as well. As I walked towards the door, it seemed to get hotter. I heard my mum shouting, 'Get out quickly!'

I ran downstairs and got to the back door, it was locked. Johnny was screaming, I put him down. I got a chair and threw it against the window and managed to open the door from the outside. I grabbed Johnny and ran out. I was free and gasping with relief.

As I collapsed on to the grass, I heard a crash as the roof caved in. I was desperate to find my parents. Inside was a pile of rubble and bricks which was once the house I lived in. I saw two images coming towards me, they were my parents. They ran to me, Mum took Johnny from me. Dad gave us a big hug, 'Thank God!' he sighed with relief . . . We were safe.

So as you can see, I lost everything, but my family looks at me as much more than just a daughter and a sister, I am a heroine.

Josie Brown (13)
Swadelands School, Kent

DOING THE DUTY

Screaming! People screaming everywhere.

Dust, fire and rubble, people everywhere trying to help. Firemen, I see, are helping a man to safety. That's all I can really see, dirt is in my eyes making it hard for me to see, but I must keep my camera focused. The world must see what has happened. I start choking in the dust, it is making my throat dry. I'm still focusing on a man being carried by firemen, it looks as though he is being carried out on a kitchen chair, his face . . . I will never forget.

The firefighters and helpers look tired and dirty, but they are doing the best they can do to help everyone. I see people running across the streets in a panic. I wish I could help, but I have to spread the news around on what a horrible thing has happened here.

Now I see that the man is safe, being looked after by the medics. Flashing lights from fire engines, ambulances and police cars, like lasers hurting my eyes. For a moment, I wished I was at home, no fear at all. My wife will be at home now, relaxing - not knowing what I am doing out here, until she turns on the news.

Jamie-Lee Ford (13)
Swadelands School, Kent

THE BOMB SHELTER

The story of my experience in the war a few years ago, fills me with happiness and sadness. This is my story . . .

A young evacuee came to stay with us today, his name is Michael and he is from Central London. We seem to get along quite well. My wife made us lovely bacon sandwiches for dinner.
'Thank you Susie,'
'You're welcome Edward, I'm going to stock up the shelter since there is going to be an air raid tonight,' she said and waddled off.

'In the shelter!' she screamed. I heard the buzz of the bombers flying overhead and the air raid siren started to bellow its cry. I ran through the house, turning the lights off.
'I'll do that Ed, go and look after the boy, I've got to get something!'
'all right, but please hurry,' I said.

Our back garden was practically a field and it took a while to get to the shelter. I was just in when *boom!* A bomb dropped at the top of the field and a woman's voice screamed in pain.

'Susie!' I hollered again and again, but no reply.
I shut the door and started blubbering like a baby and so did the boy. I was so upset.

Jonathan Lewis (13)
Swadelands School, Kent

SEA SURVIVAL

'Quick Dad. Swing down on that chain before the mast falls and hits you,' Jim shouted.

'I can't!' he said.

'Yes you can, just don't think about the height and have faith in yourself. Swing over the side and hold on, I'm coming.'

'Quick Jim, now faster. I can't hold on any longer, my hands are as cold as ice.'

'I'm coming Dad, I'm coming!'

Just as Jim got to the side of the boat, there was a great crash as a massive wave hit the ship. Jim's dad closed his eyes and said a quick prayer before he flung himself off the side of the sinking ship.

When he opened his eyes he found that he had landed with a bang in the rescue boat and into the arms of his son.

'Dad, Dad, wake up, you're with me now.'

'Thank goodness,' he said.

Then the rest of the ship went down with a gulp and hundreds of bodies floated to the surface. 'There's the man I shared a room with,' Jim's dad said, 'he was a smelly person, but okay.'

He started to row the lifeboat away and began looking for survivors at the same time. They came away from the wreckage and started to look for the American coast. Jim saw an island just a couple of miles away and decided to go and stay there until I got a signal on the SOS radio.

Jim got the signal eventually and the coastguard said that they would send a helicopter for us. The helicopter finally found the crew's smoke signals and landed on the island with a great gush of wind.

The survivors of the shipwreck got on board and the helicopter set off. America was in sight but the helicopter ran out of fuel above the Pacific.

Karim Boumnijel (13)
Swadelands School, Kent

THE HOMELESS

I love art. I always will. It's good the way you can show how you feel in a picture. Unfortunately, I won't be able to see good art anymore. You see my old boss hates me, because of what happened in 1985.

Back then, I was the newest employee of the Academy of Arts in Central London. It all started when my boss told me to order ten new gold frames.
'Herbert! Get hold of the frame company and order ten,' shouted my boss. What an idiot, I thought. Of course I would never say that out loud. This is what everyone thinks of him. I got on to the company and ordered the gold frames.

The next week the frames came - but there were 500 frames instead of ten. My boss went crazy and kicked me out of my job.
'But-but-but that means I will have no ho-home!' I said, thinking of my family.
'That's all Herbert! Now get out! by the way you have 24 hours to get out of your home!' shouted my boss.

When I got home and told my wife, she said nothing but after a while she started to cry.
'Don't worry love, it will be okay, we will get through it.'

The next day we were out - out on the street. All alone. What will we do?

Dominic Gabriel (13)
Swadelands School, Kent

ARE YOU OKAY?

The tough looking man left the saloon and started off down the busy street. As he turned the corner, a young boy saw him, he looked at him and ran away. He ran to the local shop and saw a man who was looking very distressed. The man looked up at him and tried to smile, but couldn't (I guess he was too distressed). The boy carried on walking and a man called out, 'Come in here!'
The boy walked over. 'Why?' he said.
'Don't question me!' the man said angrily, 'just come!'

The boy was very scared, he followed the man.
He walked in and the smell of cigars and beer hit him, he looked even more scared. Then the owner of the saloon came over, He said 'Are you okay?'
'Fine!' replied the boy, shaking.
He walked further in and the smell got stronger. He felt sick!

The boy decided to sit down near the back and take some deep breaths. After a while he felt worse and decided to leave, he told the man and he replied. 'Fine! I know how you must feel.'

All of a sudden, the man who seemed nice, punched the boy in the face. The boy fell on to the hard, wooden floor. Everyone was shocked and started to look worried. One man came over and he said, 'Are you alright?'
'Yes,' he replied shaking.
'I'll call for an ambulance.'

The man called for the ambulance and it took ten minutes to arrive. The boy was carried to the ambulance and the man went with him. All the way there he was sitting with the boy, talking to him. 'I feel comfortable,' said the boy.

When they got to the hospital, they went inside and the kind man told the nurse what had happened (she looked shocked!) The nurse went away and came back with some bandages. Then she started to look at his head, it was fine, just a few bruises and a big cut down his face. The boy turned - his nose, it hurt! The nurse looked at it and said, 'It's broken, but it will be okay.' She attended to the boy and he was allowed home, but he had to rest.

Four years passed and the boy was watching the news. On the news there was a shoplifter who had stolen over £100,000. He looked at the screen closely and said, 'He was the man who attacked me!'

A week later, it was on the boys information that this man had been caught. They found the money in his house and he was put in jail for life.
'Yippee!' The boy shouted at the top of his voice.

Laura Barker (13)
Swadelands School, Kent

KEEPING PEOPLE ALIVE

In the seven bedroomed house on the side of a quiet country road, lived Mr Freddy Stine.

Freddy, the 83-year-old scientist who had a laboratory in his basement, wrote down every experiment he'd ever done - from making bangs to cloning people. As he lived alone, he only had one friend, Bobo the cat. His wife had passed away a year ago, aged 79.

A kind old man was Mr Freddy Stine, but he liked to keep himself to himself. In the year 1955, he was doing a major experiment, keeping people alive. He worked in his lab 24/7 trying to make a drug to keep people alive for a long time. *Bang! Whoosh!* Went the bright orange liquid, one gulp of that and you could live for a 100 years. 'I'm done! I've done it!' shouted Freddy. He took a gulp of his powerful liquid and would wait to see if this strong stuff would work. Freddy would have to wait until he was 101 to prove that his potion would work.

He rang the local press to tell them what an amazing experiment he had made. A news reporter arrived a few hours later.
'What ingredients have you used?' he asked.
'Sorry, it's a secret . . . thank you for coming.'
Freddy thanked Mr Lloyd, the news reporter.

Mr Stine kept himself to himself for five years, no one saw or even heard of Mr Stine. The police visited him for part of another investigation and they found Mr Stine sitting in his chair, his eyes were closed, his lips were blue and his hands were cold. Not a movement did Mr Stine make.

At the age of 88, Mr Stine died of a major heart attack, no one found out whether his experiment actually worked. All we know is that he was a famous scientist and all his written experiments are in the British History Museum.

Charlotte Hemstritch (13)
Swadelands School, Kent

MY PAST

Last night I was thinking of going back to the shop where I was a boy.

It was 1939, during the war, I had been looking after my father's shop for him. When he came back he had a sad expression on his face. He said that I had to be evacuated to Wales, to go and live with a family whom I didn't know!

A week later, I finally moved away from the shop and the village and I went to Wales to live. For how long? I didn't know! It could be six months or maybe a year. I said my goodbyes and left for the train and waved from my carriage window to my parents. My mum was uncontrollably crying into a tissue.

Once I was in Wales, I wanted to go back home to England. I hated being with this strange family and there was also another person who had to be pulled away from his mum and dad. I didn't like it much.

Six months later, I've been here a while and I've received a letter from my parents. It says I can go home because it was a little safer now, but they said that we will have to move near Scotland. I wanted to go home, I was happy to see my mum and dad, but I wanted to stay at the shop and help out.

Now it's 54 years later and I'm going to see the shop again - but it might not even be there!

The shop is still there and it's quite different and empty. It would be great if I could have it like my dad had years ago. (It's got a sign on it saying *For sale!*). I wonder if I could get it and turn it into a proper house with a sweet shop. I will have to buy it.

A month later and it's a house again. It's my house and I'm going to turn it into a proper shop, a sweet shop for all the children to enjoy. When my grandchildren come over to stay, they will be able to help in the shop, just like I did with my dad.

Gemma Rogers (13)
Swadelands School, Kent

PARTY

Dad was sitting like a slug on the settee having arguments with the TV.

I'm Tracy by the way, just your average teenager. I've got a mum and a dad and brothers.

I went over to a brown box to see if there was any post. There was a pink envelope labelled *Miss Tracy Favour*. It didn't have a stamp on so it must have been delivered personally.

I ran up to my room and opened the letter it said . . .

> *Dear Tracy*
> *I would like to invite you to a surprise party*
> *for my son Derek.*

Oh no, not Derek! I haven't seen him since primary school.

I quickly ran to our old hiding place, well it wasn't exactly a hiding place, it was more of a meeting point. Derek was standing there waiting. As soon as we got re-aquainted, he invited me to a restaurant. I went home thinking, what do I wear? I opened my wardrobe and I found the perfect dress to wear. By the time I was ready, Derek had arrived and Mum was trying to get rid of us.

I had no idea where we were going. Derek said we were going to a really posh restaurant. The night was horrible, Derek's stepdad kept on commenting about me. I walked out. I didn't even bother going to his party. He's changed, we both have!

Lauren Gretton (12)
Swadelands School, Kent

THE AFTERNOON THAT STOOD STILL

A strange thing happened to me a few days ago. It was just like a dream I had once had. It all started when I was practising for an important football game.

After a long, hard, hard hour, I was getting tired, so I gave the ball one last hard kick. The ball disappeared over a large brick wall into a yellowy, browny-coloured bush.

I went out to look for the ball, but it was nowhere to be seen, but the strange thing was that everything seemed to be different. It was autumn and the trees were dark and light green, no browns, yellows or reds - just greens.

There was no one to be seen, it was deserted; no cars, no dogs barking, no planes flying overhead, just complete silence. Then I remembered it was like that dream I once had. this is a time-warp. I let out a loud scream of fright. I was scared. Am I alone? How will I get back? It's like being in a dream. Maybe if I retrace my steps I will go back.

It didn't work, I could make the most of this, I thought. I stepped inside a shop, there was no one there, I took a few chocolate bars and a video I've been wanting for ages *The Time Machine*. I stepped out and there was a sudden flash like lightning, but different! Suddenly everything was back to normal, the dogs were barking, the cars were moving, planes were in the air and the trees were brown and yellow.

Kaylie Russell (13)
Swadelands School, Kent

THE HOLIDAY

I woke up with a wet face, it was Benny on my bed. I sat up, half asleep, for a while, then I opened my eyes, I had forgotten we were going on holiday!

I went to the bathroom to brush my teeth, Benny followed me in and licked my legs. 'All right, all right, I will feed you!' I walked slowly down the stairs, swaying in a tired haze. I opened the door to the kitchen, alert to the noise. The door swung open and as I pushed it, I'd forgotten about the air vent, it was rattling. Dad hadn't had enough time to fix it before our holiday. I opened the pantry door and found a tin of dog food for Benny. I smelt it, it was half-full and it had gone off! I threw it in the bin and got another can *chicken flavour* it said on the side of the can. I realised it was a full can, I opened it, the whiff of chicken touched my nose, it was okay; I added some biscuits to the chicken and put down the bowl.

He tucked into it, I went to see the time, it was half-past eight, so I went to get out of my night-gown and change into my clothes. The suitcases were very heavy and old, Mum and Dad had used them on their honeymoon to Folkestone and they had never used them since.

We packed the night before, I opened the curtains in my room to see that the day was sunny. As it was July, it was mainly sunny. I yawned, closing my eyes as the sun beamed down and I lifted the case upwards on to its side. I pull it towards my door; I could only just move it a bit, so I tried with both arms. I finally got it to the door, and as the door was open, my dad walked by and he took it down.

Emma Foxley (13)
Swadelands School, Kent

THE BANK ROBBERY

5th July 1866, three brothers rode into town.

They had just moved into a cabin in the hills. They tied their horses up outside the saloon before going in for a drink. They sat down with their drinks and a fight started at the bar. They finished their drinks and went over to the bank where they all opened a bank account. The bank was a small building and inside there was just a desk with a safe in the corner. They put their money into their bank accounts and rode out of town . . . to rob!

They rode through the hills until they got to their cabin, their names were Bill Bob, Shane Bob and Will Bob. Will Bob made tea - beef stew. They sat around the table talking about how easy it would be to rob the bank. They decided to rob it next morning (Saturday, 6th July). The bank opened at 8am before everything else, so there wouldn't be a lot of people about.

The next morning they rode into town and tied their horses up by the side of the bank. They went in and shouted, 'This is a hold up!'
There were five people already in the bank. Will Bob got the money and jewellery off the people in the bank. Shane Bob got the money from the safe and Bill Bob kept a look-out. One of the people tried to get away, but Bill Bob shot him, they ran out and rode off, but the sheriff had just come out of his office. He shot Bill Bob in the leg and so he fell off his horse. The sheriff put him in the jail and rode off after the others.

The sheriff was however, too late, the two brothers rode off into the big sunset with Bill Bob destined for a life in jail. The other two brothers had a life of happiness.

William Viggers (12)
Swadelands School, Kent

THE MYSTERIOUS DEATH

I remember it was during the summer of 1652 when it happened.

The five of us; Rosie, Chloe, Katie, Kirsty and myself, Jessica, were down at the beach with Rosie's mum and dad.

Her dad was reading a book called *A Midsummer Night's Dream* - if you ask me, it looked really boring, one picture in the whole book!

Rosie's mum was sunbathing because it was so hot. Her long, brown curly hair, blowing in what little wind there was.

All five of us were running down to the sea, we couldn't wait to jump in. The water was so cold. So it would take us a long time to get in. We finally got in and Rosie swam on ahead of everyone else, just like normal!

First of all she lost her new hat which her grandma had bought for her a week before. So she walked in deeper to look for it. Rosie was in, up to her hips . . .

Stacey Revell (12)
Swadelands School, Kent

THE OLD CREEPY LIGHTHOUSE

It all started off when Mum said we were going on holiday to a famous old lighthouse. We thought it sounded great until Mum told us about the ghost who lived there. I was freaked out about it, but Mark thought it was the coolest thing ever to see a ghost.

We were all getting ready for bed. I went upstairs to unpack my bag and someone was turning my light on and off. I said, 'Stop it Mark, you are so annoying!' But Mum was downstairs, talking to Mark! So I screamed because it wasn't him.

They all came running up the stairs. They said, 'What have you seen?'
'A *ghost!*'
Mark said, 'Whatever. I will see the first ghost, not you!'
Mum said, 'Go and sleep in your brother's room if you're scared,'
So I did.

Then in the morning Mark, my brother, wasn't in his bed. I went and told Mum and she said, 'He's at the bottom of our bed.'
I went round saying, 'Mark is a scaredy-cat!'
We both told Mum we had seen a ghost, but Mum didn't believe us.

We went home early because Mark and I didn't want to stay another minute in the lighthouse. Mum said, 'You both have wild imaginations about ghosts.'

In the end, Mum didn't believe us, but we knew it was true.

Sam Rose (13)
Swadelands School, Kent

MOLLY'S SECRET

'What shall I do?' I whispered to myself. 'I'm so scared.'
'Molly, what are you doing up there? Come down here now.'
I could tell Mum was drunk because she was slurring.

'If I have to come up there and get you, you're dead!' she shouted.
I was so scared. What was she going to do to me, I didn't know?
Cautiously I started towards the stairs. She stood at the bottom with a
bottle of Bacardi Breezer in her hand. In the other hand she had a
cigarette, I could tell by the way she looked that she'd been to the pub. I
could even smell it on her.

'Come here, I've got £5 in my hand that you have to take with you
today. You will have to get a bus to town, or start walking. You've got
a list of what to get me?' she slurred. 'But remember if you come back
without *all* my shopping, you really will wish that you'd got it all.' As I
slipped past her, I was shaking.
'Okay Mum!' I sighed.

Once clear of her, I began to run as fast as my little legs would go.
'Don't forget all my shopping' she shouted after me.
'Okay Mum!'
Luckily my bus was there waiting, when I got there.

When I finally reached the town I jumped off the bus, but the bus driver
called me back.
'What are you doing on your own? Where are your parents? Do they
know where you are? Are you lost?' He asked so many questions.
'No, I'm on my own because my mother asked me to get her a few
things.'
'How old are you?'
'Five' I answered very quietly.

I ran towards the centre of town just as he looked shocked and said,
'Five!'

Then I noticed a man selling his possessions on the street and I watched him silently. I noticed that he was watching me too. I couldn't believe it, it was my Grandad Albert. I ran into his arms.

I started telling him about Mum, how she'd just come back from the pub. I told him everything. He said he would tell the police about her beating me.
'No!' I shouted at him.
'Why, you can't hide it. I have to tell them. If I do you can stay with me and everything will be fine.' He tried to convince and comfort me.
'Please!' he assured me.

'Hello!' I called, 'I have all the shopping you wanted.'
I was now at home, 'Mum, are you there?'

'In here,' my mum answered.
I walked into the living room where my mum was sitting with the police.
'What are you doing?' I asked.
'They want to take you away from me!'
I could tell she'd been crying.
The police woman put her hand on my shoulder. 'It'll be all right,' she said. 'It's for the best!'

Jade Bell (13)
Swadelands School, Kent

I'LL MISS YOU

'You'll be fine once I'm gone,' Henry mumbled. 'I'll make sure the
child benefit arrives so you'll have nothing to worry about.'
'There's the truck, you'd better go. I wish you didn't have to go though.
Have you got your toothbrush? I think you've left your comb upstairs.'
I said worriedly.
Would I cope on my own? I asked myself.

'Really! I'm fine, stop worrying about me! Bye!' Henry cried.
I gave him one last hug, my hands gripping his body so tight that it
could cut off his circulation.
'Goodbye!' I replied 'I'll miss you.'

I watched the truck pull away - I waved to my beloved husband. I made
sure he remembered me with a smiling face - not tears. After all, I
wanted to be strong for him and I would take the best care of our son.

Chloe Osborne (12)
Swadelands School, Kent

RANSOM CHASE

'Look what you've done!'
'Sorry, I'll go and get more.'

Monday morning and Kirsty had spilt the milk. Putting on her mum's slippers, Kirsty slunk to the shops.

The eerie street was unusually quiet and Kirsty was sure she heard footsteps, but she wanted to get home quickly. Suddenly a hand grabbed her around the mouth. In shock she dropped her milk as she was dragged down the dark alley.

'Where is she?' complained Sean. Kirsty had been gone too long, so Sean set out to find her. Before long, Sean found a pile of broken glass and a puddle of milk flowing down into the gutter. Sean noticed a note on a brick explaining that Kirsty was being held ransom for £10,000.

Worried for his sister's safety he ran home with the note to tell his mum.
'We need to tell the police,' said their mum running to the phone. Trudging back she whimpered, 'The police won't help us, not since your father robbed that bank.'

Sean and his mum quickly gathered the ransom into a briefcase. Sean had built a tracking device which he hid in the case. He also had a can of nerve gas.

The ransom was left at the pick-up point and a man ran past, tossing a beaten Kirsty to the ground, then grabbed the ransom. As the kidnapper took off, Sean was in hot pursuit. The kidnapper ran down a blocked alley, so Sean tossed the can of nerve gas at him and caught the kidnapper. Kirsty was safe and Sean was a hero.

Matthew Beaumont (13)
Swadelands School, Kent

NEVER ALONE

Some girls think they have the answers to everything, but one particular girl didn't . . .

Paige Brown had an extraordinary problem, she had an inner person inside her who had a frightful soul . . .

'Leave me alone, get out of me!' screamed Paige.

Suddenly a girl named Brook walked in and looked at Paige. Eventually she plucked up the courage to ask her what was wrong, but unfortunately the voice spoke out.
'Don't listen to her! she's evil, evil I say!'

Luckily before Paige could react again Brook took her hand to sit her down.
'Tell me Paige, what's wrong?' asked Brook. 'You don't look yourself!'
Soon after, *It* started to repeat.
'She's evil, evil I say!'

Paige jumped up, hit Brook and ran out holding a hand to her head, crying.
Brook came running out with watery eyes.
'Don't cry Paige, tell me!' The voice was still whispering.

'I talk to myself, I have a voice in my head,' Paige sobbed '*It* tells me I'm evil, I'm not, all I want are friends!'
'I'm your friend, no way are you evil. You're so kind! Anyway, it's normal for people to talk to themselves!'

'No, but this voice has an accent, it's not English, it's Irish I think. I'm English,' sniffed Paige.
'I'll tell you what, let's go out and forget about it,' suggested Brook.

Paige and Brook had a fab day, riding roller coasters, going to the circus and loads more.
'Brook! Brook!' called Paige 'I think *It's* gone!'

Kayleigh Hopkinson (13)
Swadelands School, Kent

PRIVATE HILL

I was always scared of my father. There was something wrong with him but mother never admitted it, he used to beat my mother and I. I couldn't talk to anyone, I had no friends because I didn't go to school. We could afford private tutoring.

Whenever I was upset about what father did, I would run up to my private hill. I would always hop over the fence and run to a pile of rocks under which was my life. My red scratched diary in which I write all my problems. Father was on every page. As I was writing I would sit on the hill, looking at the crystal blue ocean.

On an early morning in August another argument, I knew that it was mother and father, so I dressed in old clothes and ran to my private hill. As usual I looked for my diary but to my horror it was gone! I heard chuckling behind me, I turned round and saw a pale boy and in his feeble hand I saw my diary. As rage filled up in my stomach, a fray of my short, red hair waved across my eyes. I brushed it away, but the boy had gone.

Weeks later I still didn't have my diary back, but the shock happened in September when my father went missing. My mother wasn't getting worried.

Weeks later mother and I were moving house. For the last time I went to visit my private hill to say goodbye. As I sat on the hill looking at the seagulls diving into the ocean, I heard chuckling, I turned around and there, smiling, was the boy, but he was pointing to a grave, it was his grave! I stared and then realised he'd read my diary about my problems with father. He made him go missing! I smiled and then heard my mother's voice calling, 'Come on, get in the car.' I ran to the car and saw that the boy had disappeared leaving my diary on the long grassland.

Eleanor Rawson (12)
Swadelands School, Kent

UNEXPECTED MURDER

One day a girl called Claire was visiting her friend. When it was time to go home, she left and met her boyfriend halfway.

They were both on their way home and suddenly they bumped into George, her ex-boyfriend. Claire cried and went bright red.
Tom said, 'What's up?'
She said, 'George was my ex-boyfriend and I dumped him for you.'
George heard what she said and stomped off in total disgust.

So Claire and Tom carried on home. They reached Claire's house and Tom gave her a kiss and went home.

It was the next day, Claire went into town with her mum, then off to Asda to shop. When they got into Asda, Claire met her nan and went to stay round her house. She had pizza and stayed to watch a DVD. It was a blast! The next day she walked home with her friend Sarah.

Because it was such a long way, they stopped at Bella's sweetshop and went to the park. They walked back and Sarah went off to her house. Claire carried on and came face to face with George but he had a knife.

She ran. He ran - then she ran into the toilets and so did he!
Suddenly . . . 'Arghhh!'

Amy Dale (12)
Swadelands School, Kent

MY FIRST TIME

My footprints made a crack across the dew on the grass as my dad and I approached the van. We got my new yellow quad, with a big number one on the front, out of the shed. I undid the chain and rolled it up the ramp into the van.

It took us about an hour to get there. The traffic was not too bad. When we got to the race track Dad parked the van up and got my quad out. He got it checked over by one of the marshalls. It was okay. My first race was in 20 minutes. I got all my race gear on, ready to go.

Dad started my quad up and warmed it up. I was getting more and more nervous, it was my first race ever. The marshall put the 15 second board up. I was getting more nervous. Then he put the five second board up, the gates went down, it was go, go, go!

I came into the first corner well, I was in about ninth place. Then over a jump, someone had overtaken me in the air. On the last lap I got him back. Over all, I came in ninth, I was very pleased.

The big day was still to come because I still had two races left. They would be the next weekend. On the Sunday, Dad did some modifications to my quad, so that it would go quicker next weekend.

Guy Raines (13)
Swadelands School, Kent

SEA OF MEMORIES

I had to go. I couldn't stand it anymore. I don't know why I came to the sea in the first place. Maybe it was because I thought that he would be here. I hoped that maybe he was still alive, but he's not.

I stripped down to my swimming suit. This was the first time I had been down to the sea since the accident. The weather was hot and I could feel the warmth of the sun on my back. That was the first time, the first moment since the accident, the first moment in the water, it made me shudder. It was cold and I nervously tiptoed forward. As I bent over to put my hands in the water, a colourful beach ball hit me in the face. I threw it back to the little girl, she smiled sweetly, but I was still sad and didn't smile back. I tried to walk on but my legs froze. I saw something in the water. I slowly walked towards it but it was drifting further away.

Soon I was up to my waist and the object had disappeared. I panicked, I felt the sand give way under my feet. It felt like someone was pulling me down. I could feel the water rising.

Tracey Washington (13)
Swadelands School, Kent

THE BOMB MASTER

Once, a man called Neil bombed a nightclub with his brother and got arrested . . .

Two brothers called Neil and Sam weren't too keen on a few people. Therefore, they decided to follow them.

One night they went in a nightclub called Fab. Neil had a plan because he didn't really like Jim and Bob. Neil decided to bomb the whole nightclub. Sam, Neil's brother, said, 'I will put a bomb in a bottle with nails in it. It will explode and go into their eyes.'

On the following Friday, Sam went there with the bottle and left it on the side. After Sam left Fab they counted down, 10, 9, 8, 7, 6, 5, 4, 3, 2, 1, bombs away! The whole, entire nightclub blew up.

The brothers weren't too sure if Jim and Bob were dead. A few minutes later the police and firefighters came. Neil asked, 'What is going on, how many people have died?'
The police said, 'About ten people have died and five injured.'
Neil asked, 'Do you know what the people who died look like?'
The police described all the ten people but none of them sounded like Jim and Bob. Neil told Sam and they both thought that Jim and Bob had got away and hadn't died. Luckily, only a tiny little bit of the building was gone.

After two years, Neil and Sam got arrested. Then Neil had a plan and he escaped. Neil didn't have anywhere to go and he was found on the streets.

In the end, Fab changed into a police station.

Pao Yin Wong (12)
Swadelands School, Kent

BUNKING

It was in 1990 that it happened. I decided to get up out of bed, I opened my window and it was raining hard. There was very thick fog. I decided to bunk off school with my mate, Daniel.

At eight o'clock I left for school. When I got there I said to Daniel, 'Do you want to bunk?'
'Yes,' he said, so we went down to the skatepark.

We were very bored. Daniel said we could go back to his house. We went back to Daniel's house. When we got there we got some food and drink and left to go back to the skatepark. When we got back all the fog had gone. James decided to jump to impress his friends. No one could watch him. He landed on his foot, he could not walk. We had to call an ambulance and when it came, we took him to hospital. He had an X-ray and it showed that he had broken his leg. We phoned his mum and dad and they came straight away and took him home.

They grounded him for months and months. When he was allowed out again he went down to the skatepark and everybody was laughing at him and told him he couldn't skate. James started skating in the smaller skatepark. He fell over and cut his knee. He went home crying and said to his mum, 'I want to move.'

James was never seen again.

James Andrews (13)
Swadelands School, Kent

DEATH

Death, we don't know much about it, it also has different names. For example: dead, no longer alive, deceased, left the station, departed.

The one thing we do know about it is that it brings loneliness. One man who knows a lot about this is Margaret (weird I know). Here's his story.

It was the hottest day so far. Everything was fine. Margaret and Kimmie had been married for six months. This wasn't the first time for Margaret, he had been married before. He had a first love, Joanne. They had been married for 40 years and after she died he thought he would never find love again. Oh boy was he wrong.

The local old folk's community centre was holding an antiques fair. There were old people but weirdly enough, young people as well, a bit like bingo!

That's where they met. They got talking and found out that they liked the same things. One thing was that he was 70 and she was 21. You would think the age gap would put them off but no! They were acting like lovesick puppies, *Ugh!* They had been together for a month, when Margaret decided to ask for Kimmie's hand in marriage.

11 months on and everything was fine until after they had gone to the park. They crossed the road and Kimmie accidentally dropped her bag. Along came a lorry and knocked her onto the pavement.

Days went past and there was no improvement. Margaret couldn't stand it, he went home and took an overdose. One hour later, after they had found him, Kimmie woke up.

Kimmie got all his money. We know that's what she wanted anyway. Oh, and did I tell you why his name was Margaret? Well, his parents wanted a girl but had him instead, *shame!*

Annabel Brand (13)
Swadelands School, Kent

THE BILLY CONNOLLY STORY

Hello, I'm Billy Connolly. I've got long, fizzy, blond hair and a grey, itchy beard. I'm very tall, as high as a door. I've been divorced three times and married three times to the same woman, I don't know why. I live in a flat in a dump called London. I used to live in a nice house but I don't now because of the television business going down the drain.

In 1997 on 1st October it happened, the day I dreaded, the day I didn't want to be alive, the day I got fired because I was too old. I wasn't funny anymore.

Before I got fired I married Jordan three times all the same way, same church, same food and the same reception.

I've got a new job as a pre-school teacher. It doesn't pay like television pays. I get better holidays at school, but television's more fun than saying 'Two times two is four'.

I did the Lotto. As per usual, the same numbers - 3, 12, 21, 34, 46, 22. I never win, except for tonight! They came out, 12, 21, 3, 21, 34, 46 and the bonus ball, 22. I was just about to rip it up then I thought, they're my numbers. They said it is estimated that there's one winner who's got £20 million. That should get me back into showbusiness and the television business.

I got married once again to Jordan, in the same place and at the same time.

Jack Ambrose (13)
Swadelands School, Kent

WORLD CUP '98

Last night I dreamt of winning the World Cup for England, but then I woke up because today I'm going to see England play in the World Cup with my friends, Sam, Guy and Will. This year it's being played in France and me and the lads were really excited. We couldn't wait for it to get on the way because everyone in England thought that it was England's year.

We arrived at the airport and within half an hour we were there, in France. Sam and Guy couldn't wait to get into the French pubs but Will and me could. England's match was tomorrow and we were so nervous that we couldn't even drink. It was midnight here in France, so we made our way to our first hotel which was in Lyon.

It was about 9am in the morning. England's first match was at 11am. We made our way to the stadium. There were already 2,000 people screaming their heads off watching England train.

England's first match was against Tunisia. It was about to kick-off. England took an early throw towards Paul Scholes and he scored. Just before half-time Alan Shearer doubled the lead. The final score was 2-0 to England. Sam, Guy, Will and me were so pleased with our country's performance we all went and got drunk.

It was Wednesday, England's next match and we lost 2-1 against Romania. All of us were very unhappy. We were getting really nervous for the next match because if we lost we would go out. If we won, however, we would go through to play Argentina.

We beat Columbia 2-0 and went through to play the mighty Argentina. Sam and Guy said, 'I bet we lose.'

It was 7pm and the match was on the way. It was full-time and 2-2. It went into penalty shoot-out and we lost. Sam was upset. The police came and arrested him. The rest of the boys and me waited for him overnight. We got out and went home and Sam felt better for seeing his family. I said, 'Never mind, maybe next time.'

Chris Holmes (13)
Swadelands School, Kent

MESSAGE IN A BOTTLE

It seemed like the perfect holiday, sunbathing in Tenerife with my friends, but while I was getting a tan, I didn't know that this was going to be a holiday to remember . . .

I was sunning myself on the beach, snoring on a beach towel, while my friends were surfing. I was awoken from my dreams by a rumble, like thunder. I jumped up and shouted, 'Come in!' to my friends. Then I saw it - a huge wave rising up from the sea on the horizon . . . I knew what this meant, *'Tidal wave!'* I bellowed.

My friends instantly ran to shore. 'We must get to safety Matt,' my friend cried, 'and quick!' she added.
'B-b-but w-w-where?' I asked, looking around in a panic.
'Up there!' She pointed to a lighthouse on the cliff.
I didn't like the idea of climbing but it was a far better idea than taking our chances here.

We started the long, hard trek up the cliff. It was a hard climb. My knees scraped on the slippery rocks, twice I lost my grip but was caught by my friend. Finally, tired, cut and bruised, we scrambled into the lighthouse.

We didn't know how long it was until all went calm, but from the clifftop we watched the sea settle. When all was well we went down to the beach again. I was just about to take a nap when . . .
'Come over here, Matt, now!'
I groaned and stumbled up as my friend called me over. 'There,' she said. She pointed at a bottle lying in the sand. The bottle had a slip of paper inside. *Help, help me* was written on it. I picked up the bottle, we looked at each other. 'Well what do you think about that?' my friend asked.
'Don't know,' I answered, 'but someone definitely needed our help!'

Emma Miles (13)
Swadelands School, Kent

THE GREAT WHITE

It was a horrible day, that gruesome, life-taking day. I remember that day in 1836, the 1st of October. The worst day of my life and others in fact. It was a stupid risk we made on that very disastrous day. We saw the storm but we never turned around. I knew it was a big mistake.

On that day it was a misty, warm morning as I woke up at 4 o'clock. We all got on that faithful fishing ship. My friends - Joe, William and Aaron and I were looking forward to catching fish, but we didn't know what was waiting for us. My friends and I had something in common - we liked doing the same things like fishing, especially William. We also both had blue eyes.

As I said, it was a very bright, warm, sunny day when we launched off to sea, heading into the Atlantic Ocean. Time flew by, we caught some fish and we were far enough out in the ocean. But people wanted to go even further out into the ocean to catch bigger fish and so we did!

A massive storm came over the horizon. You could see the deadly waves from where we were. The storm was heading for us but we still kept on going, thinking it would clear. The storm was close. We reeled our nets in, in case the storm ripped them. We all hoped for the best!

Suddenly, something pulled the net under the boat. A huge shudder then a crash. There was a hole in the bottom of the boat, the boat was sinking! The storm was above us. Huge waves were hitting the front of the boat. The engines eventually were destroyed so we couldn't get away. We abandoned ship! All the lifeboats had been crushed where the mast had hit them, except for two boats, so me and others escaped.

Many people died. We felt hurt. The others that escaped started new lives and different jobs but were scarred from that day. That day will never leave me.

Shane Tuffey (13)
Swadelands School, Kent

THE ATTACK

My name is Williams, Rupert Williams. I am 76 years of age and I live in New York City. I suffer from heart problems and have already had two attacks.

I was in my flat, alone as usual. I had just cooked and eaten my dinner. I suddenly smelt burning. I checked that the cooker was off and it was. I walked into the living room and the smell got stronger. I looked out of the window and immediately saw the huge commotion coming from below, a fire and it was spreading fast! I panicked. Then, that feeling in my chest, I knew what it meant. My balance was going, everything went blurry. I felt as if I were reeling, spinning. I was so dizzy that I felt sick. I knew exactly what was about to happen. I quickly gasped for air, but just felt myself slowly falling, falling, falling.

'Good morning Mr Williams, how do you feel? Please take these pills and I'll pop in to check on you in a while.' It was a nurse. Everything was still a bit hazy but I realised I was in a hospital bed. It was warm and soft, unlike my hard mattress at home. There was a strange banging inside my head.

Suddenly, Rina Brown, a neighbour of mine, came and sat beside me. She told me how I was unconscious and the New York Fire Department rescued me just before the fire spread into my home. I realised that I had nothing left. Seeing as I had no family or friends, I expected to be alone in the world until Rina kindly offered for me to stay with her at her mother's until I could sort something out. I happily agreed.

Although I had lost my home and belongings, I had gained some friends. I now realise that I should appreciate life much more.

Katie Simpson (13)
Swadelands School, Kent

AT THE SEASIDE

20th July 1965

It was a Saturday morning and we, the Brooks family, were going to the beach. We got ready and got in the car. Eventually we got there.

The beach was full of people. Luckily, Mum found a space for us to sit. We laid out the mat and sat under the umbrella. We went into the water. Mary didn't like it because her hat kept blowing off and getting wet. Mum called us over to get some food. We had cheese sandwiches and orange squash. After that we all helped to make a sandcastle. Charlotte, Julie and me made the sandcastle and Mary and Cynthia made the moat. The tide was coming in quickly so Mum took us to get an ice cream. Then we packed up our stuff and said goodbye to the sandcastle we'd made.

On the way back home, Mary started to cry because she noticed her dolly wasn't there and she had left it at the beach. She cried so much Mum said she would buy her a new one. Mum bought us some fish and chips. On the way out of the shop, Cynthia dropped her chips all over the floor. I had to share mine with her.

I hope we can go back soon, it was fun on the beach. We had collected some sea shells, we counted them and put them on our drawers in the bedroom. Goodnight.

Lucy Missing (12)
Swadelands School, Kent

THE EVIL ZOMBIE

Nemesis, an evil zombie has thought of a plan to take over the world. He says to his zombie slaves, 'Go around the world turning the world leaders into zombies.'

M16 satellites pick up the plans to take over the world and they send the pictures to M16 headquarters. At first they take it as a joke but when India's king gets zombified, they take it pretty seriously.

'We've got to do something,' said Tony Blair, frustrated, 'get me Buffy's brother, Blade, the zombie slayer, now!'
'Yes Sir,' said Sergeant Mean sternly, 'I'll go now Mr Blair.'
'Thank you sergeant,' said Mr Blair.

Meanwhile Nemesis was planning an attack on President Bush. 'We shall attack at midnight,' shouted Nemesis to his zombie followers. 'Yes Sir!' they all shouted and prepared for quite a hard fight. They got tools, axes, chainsaws and shotguns and went to the underground tunnels to America. They waited until President Bush went to his bedroom, then they could strike.

'Goodnight honey,' said Mrs Bush.
'Goodnight dear,' replied Mr Bush.
The zombies didn't waste their chance. They bashed through the floor and started attacking Mr Bush. *'Ahhhh heeelp me!'* screamed the president.

Just then there was a massive crash, then Blade came through the roof.
'Who the hell are you?' said one zombie, puzzled.
'Oh, so zombies can speak now,' said Blade, 'where's Nemesis?' he shouted.
'Hey, you didn't answer my question,' said the zombie, annoyed.
'I'm your worst nightmare,' laughed Blade.
'What Blade? I thought Nemesis . . .'
Before he could say anything else Blade blew his head off. 'If any other zombie wants to be decapitated, please come here,' said Blade sarcastically.

All the zombies charged at him. Before they could even get close, Blade blew their heads off.

'Are you okay Mr President?'
'Yes, thanks to you, Blade.'
'It was my pleasure,' said Blade.
'But how do you do it Blade?' said Mr Bush.
'I am one of them,' said Blade sadly.
'What do you mean?' said Mr Bush.
'You'll see,' Blade laughed and he ran off through the door.

'Well done Blade,' said Tony Blair joyfully, 'but you've still got Nemesis to handle.'
'He'll be easy,' said Blade.
'I hope so Blade,' said Tony Blair, a bit worried.
'Don't worry too much,' said Blade, who then walked off to get Nemesis.

Blade went to the White House to see if he could get to Nemesis by going through the hole they made. Sure enough it went for miles and it stank of rotting flesh and bones. When Blade got to the end of the tunnel he couldn't believe his eyes. There was a mass of zombies and weapons as well as chainsaws. It was zombie heaven. Blade didn't waste his chance, he got his grenade launcher and shot every way possible. The zombies went mad and then amongst the explosions . . . Nemesis! 'Leave him to me,' shouted Nemesis, 'I thought I'd zombified you Blade!'
'You did, but I escaped with a minor bite which was treated,' said Blade.
'Damn you Blade,' replied Nemesis.
'Damn this Nemesis,' laughed Blade and he got out a chain gun. *Dagadagadadaga.* As it ran out of bullets, Nemesis lay there with masses of holes. 'You thought that would stop me Blade,' laughed Nemesis.
'No, but it distracted you,' said Blade.
'What!' said Nemesis.
'I put the gun down while it was shooting and I planted a nuke on you,' laughed Blade.

'What?' shouted Nemesis.
'Goodbye Nemesis,' Blade said sarcastically and he ran off, out of the way of danger . . . *boom!*

Blade went to check it out. They found traces of other zombies but not of Nemesis, the chaos was over.
'Well, that's what they think, ha-ha-ha,' said a voice.

Jay Broster (13)
Swadelands School, Kent

LONDON'S BURNING

'Watch out it's going to come down!'
Everybody turned and just like that, sparks of fire went everywhere.
Suddenly people were screaming and sirens were heard from the pub a
mile down the road. Within two minutes the roof of the burning house
fell in. People watched as the building fell down and a nearby car
exploded.

Gary looked as his flat fell to the ground. *Smash!* It was too late,
Bluebell village was choked with smoke.

It was all my fault he thought as he ran to a nearby hotel. It was me who
caused the fire, the smoke, the shame.

Some time later Gary returned to what had been his house. As he
crossed the road his mum said, 'Where the hell have you been? I
thought you were dead.'
'It's my fault, I took a cigarette.'
'Ahh, you did what?'
'You heard, a cigarette.'
'Why?'
'I don't know Mum.'
'You know you shouldn't have.'

Tom Weeks (13)
Swadelands School, Kent

BEND IT LIKE JENNY

I stepped out onto my garden, just me, Jenny Thompson, and my football. I placed the ball down and thought of David Beckham and how much I wanted to be a footballer (even though I wasn't very good at it). I saw my goalpost at the bottom of the garden and used the washing line as a wall. I ran up to the ball and hit it cleanly. As I watched I realised. I realised I could become a pro as I watched the ball fly round and over the washing line, swerve back in and hit the top corner. Every one of them went exactly the same way.

The next day was the first day of a tournament for Tanfield Rangers who were the local team playing in the London Cup. I woke up, got dressed and ran downstairs. My dad said to me, 'Now don't worry if you don't get a game in this tournament,' thinking we were going to go out.

When we got there my coach said I was going to be sub. As I was the worst player I expected it. The game was bleak apart from the fact that I got brought on and scored from inside my own half.

In other games we walked it through, scoring twelve and letting in seven, as we charged through to the final.

On the morning of the final I was told there would be scouts from all over the country. To add to the tension, it was being played at Wembley. I felt an odd feeling in my stomach. What if I didn't play well, what would happen?

The game kicked off and the other team literally went and scored and scored again until the end of the first half.

I got out for the second half and felt I needed to do something about it and before I touched the ball we got a free kick. I quickly ran up to the ball, hit it and chipped it over the goalkeeper. Next minute, I crossed the ball in and Laura headed it in.

With minutes remaining we won another free kick. I swerved it round the wall and towards goal and Becky Jones volleyed it in.

Greenock 2 - 3 Tanfield Rangers

It was one of the best moments of my life, I felt so glad. We celebrated all over the pitch and to top if off I got trials for Man U and England.

Luke Stanley (13)
Swadelands School, Kent

SPOOKED

Hugo was a jolly old man at the grand old age of seventy-five. Everyone knew him and everyone liked him, but at one point in his life he changed. He became scared and shy. The only one who knows why is him.

Hugo woke up in the early hours of the morning. He went to the pub the night before and had a terrible hangover. Hugo needed to go shopping, but he only had a little bit of money. After he came home from shopping, Hugo made himself a cup of tea. He started watching BBC1, but fell asleep halfway through a programme.

Smash! Hugo woke suddenly. He checked his watch: 1.30am. Hugo wondered what had happened, then he heard a creaking noise. He got out of bed then went downstairs. He saw some saucepans on the floor, so he decided to ring the police, but it was hours before they came round.

Hugo was asleep (as usual) when he heard a knock on the door. 'Shut up,' he yelled. It wouldn't stop, so, reluctantly Hugo got out of bed, and the second he did, it stopped.
'Aaarrrggghhh!' Bang! Hugo heard a massive scream . . .

Jack Rose (13)
Swadelands School, Kent

THE BOAT CRASH

As I walked down the side of the boat, the man at the top rang the bell for 10pm. I was supposed to meet my brother for dinner that night. We hadn't seen each other for ages, well not properly anyway. There were lots of shouts from the captain's bridge, which was just down the boat.

Suddenly, *bang!* I found myself hanging at the edge of the boat holding on for my life. I was scared, really scared. My hands were red and my face was pale and I had blood pouring down my face. People and their children were crying. You could see the look on their faces, the look that said their time could be up. As I tried to get to the top of the boat, it started to pour down with rain. the noise of the waves crashing against the boat was thundering. There were people falling off, I mean just little kids. It's still quite scary to think about it. I still have nightmares.

I managed to stumble onto a lifeboat along with some others, but my brother was not so lucky. I was going to try to jump in and get him, but it was too late for my brother. I felt that it was my fault he died on that boat.

Adam Overs (13)
Swadelands School, Kent

DO UFOS REALLY EXIST?

Yesterday a UFO was seen landing in the main part of Windsor at 12 midnight. A woman named Christina Hornby, sighted this.

This is her description of the actual so-called spaceship: 'It was about as big as my house and on the outside it had SS Earth on the side, and also on that side, it had some gross bluey-green goo coming out. It was disgusting.

I was just walking down Sheet Street and I saw this big, blinding light and I looked up once the light had faded and I saw a giant spaceship. If you don't believe me, you can ask my friend who was with me at the time'.

This is what her friend said: 'We were going down the long walk and we were going to see our old school, Brigidine and then there was a blinding light. I could barely see where I was going. When the light had ended, we looked up and saw a humungous spaceship. On the sides it had disgusting goo coming out from a loose place in the ship which was horrid'.

Thank you Samantha and Christina. We will hear more about that later.

Christina Hornby (12)
The Brigidine School, Berkshire

THE IVORY ELEPHANT

'I brought it back from Varanissa when I returned from India last year. I'm going to give it to you, Amanda and Joe, as a wedding present.' The old man held out the gift. Everyone gasped . . . it was an exquisite ivory elephant with amber eyes that glittered mysteriously . . .

Thirteen years later, Damien, Amanda and Joe's twelve-year-old son, was flicking through their photo album. One picture particularly took his attention, that of Amanda holding a small elephant. Curious, Damien asked what had become of the carving. On being directed to a trunk of Eastern design in the attic, Damien fumbled in the gloom through its contents. Then the glittering amber eyes met his and, on being touched, a small, ivory elephant emitted a strange, mystical tune.

Later that year, the family visited the little Indian village of Varanissa, the original home of the carved elephant, so Damien took the statue with him.

One night, whilst dining with a family friend, Professor Nikaren, Damien produced the elephant. The Indian man's face blanched. 'Where did you get that?' he murmured. 'Fourteen years ago that was stolen from the temple of Kali. Earthquakes, floods and famines followed. It must be returned at once!'

Outside, Damien cycled furiously through the night, his heartbeat fast as he approached the temple with its awesome stature of Kali. Summoning all his courage, he placed the elephant on the altar. A low, shuddering sigh followed and Damien felt as though his mission had been truly accomplished.

Harriet Mallinson (11)
The Brigidine School, Berkshire

DOWNWARDS

She had arrived. Mr Matthews sighed. He could hear the roar of the Rolls Royce swinging into the car park of the Hotel de Ville. He sank back into the soft, red armchair in the lobby as if he could avoid the impending meeting. Everything in this hotel was red. The staff were dressed smartly in their red uniform, the colour of blood. The lawyer did not like this hotel at all. It made him feel uneasy. Two huge stone dragons crouched at the entrance, watching over the whole hotel. He did not like the staff either. They would walk past him and whisper to each other, which made him nervous.

Not that he wasn't already nervous. Mr Matthews trembled as she stormed in through the revolving glass doors. Her sparkling black shoes tapped the polished red floor as she took each step. Her marching footsteps echoed around the silent hotel. He watched her sequinned dress glitter in the bright lights as she swept it around her. Her expensive fur coat was thrown at a porter without a second glance as she proceeded angrily towards him. What could she want now?

'I want to amend my will!' Lady Worthington was giving orders. Her lawyer sighed again. The old woman was always making a fuss. He felt sorry for her children. She had never loved them, never given them any money. They had deserted her as soon as they could. Lady Worthing continued her instructions. ' I want to remove any possessions I left to my son, Arthur, sneaky, good-for-nothing boy. Always pestering me about this, that and the other, and as for that wife of his . . .' Mr Matthews held up his hand to silence her. He had heard enough of the tirade already. He had met Arthur Worthington and had liked him very much. The lawyer knew that he would only approach his mother if it was important.

Mr Matthews looked at the sky outside. The soft red light of the evening sun had faded away behind the rolling hills that loomed in the distance. The rising moon lit up the countryside with silvery light. Tonight was the full moon, shining above the trees. Moonbeams shone down onto Mr Matthews' car. It was getting late. He really needed to get back to the office. 'Very well, I will get back to you in the morning.' He stuffed his notes into his briefcase and headed for the door. Lady Worthington sniffed and made her way to reception.

'The Imperial Suite, Madam? Floor 10 on the left.' The receptionist pointed at the lift as she handed over the keys.
'Let me escort you, Madam,' the manager, dressed in a blood-red top hat and tail coat, stood right beside her, before moving swiftly away towards the lift. As they drew closer, the doors glided open. Lady Worthington stepped into the lift at the same moment as hundreds of other Lady Worthingtons, reflected in the mirrored walls, scowled back. The lift started. There was no jolt, no creak, just a smooth and soundless movement, downwards, downwards, downwards.

A thought struck Lady Worthington suddenly. 'I was told the Imperial Suite was on the tenth floor. We should be going up.'
'It is,' replied the manager, 'but you're not going there.' He lifted his hat to show two shiny, red horns poking from his greasy, black hair. 'You're coming with me.'

Catriona Shearer (12)
The School of St Helen & St Katharine, Oxfordshire

IS THERE A CURE FOR HELEN'S HOPPING?

Just try to get your head round this one.

At lunchtime on Monday 12th March, most people were having a normal lunch, in the usual way. Helen Brown's mealtime, however, was not turning out so well. Helen (aged 13 years) attended St Trinian's School near Abingdon. At this dreaded lunchtime, she suddenly turned into an ugly brown frog. 'I was gobsmacked,' Lizzy Smith told us. 'I was just sitting there next to Helen, eating my lunch as I always do. Then I looked away. When I looked back, there she was, sitting on the table croaking at me!'

Apparently Lizzy quickly ate the rest of her lunch and bundled the frog into her lunch box. She thinks her best friend was eating spinach sandwiches as usual but when asked about what could have happened, she just shrugged her shoulders and looked sad.

Mrs Brown acted surprisingly calmly when she was told the strange and almost impossible story of her daughter's transformation. She describes herself as 'coping well under the tragic circumstances'. Apparently she has kept the frog. The amphibian has a little bed in the living room. For sheets she has her father's hankies and for a bed, a box. When asked what she had thought when she had first seen the ugly little frog, Mrs Brown answered, 'When I looked into her eyes and she croaked, it sounded just like 'Mummy'.'

The day after this horrific incident, Lizzy has been reported to have visited the science teacher, Mrs Johnson, with the strange creature in her lunch box. 'I was astonished I had never seen such a specimen like this before, so of course, I wanted to keep it'. We asked if the frog had looked at all human. The answer was, 'Yes . . . now you come to mention it . . . she did. her mouth looked slightly human proportioned'. There is no scientific reason for this strange and unexpected change, but there have been rumours that it was set up as a joke by Helen herself. She could have run away, leaving on the table, a frog out of the school pond to scare her friend.

However the amphibian expert that Lizzy also went to see disagrees with these rumours, saying that people would have seen Helen slip away. The expert, Mr Welch, described this as an excellent specimen of the. ordinary garden frog 'I was really disappointed when I was told I couldn't keep it for tests'. Brian Welch thought that this was probably caused, if anything, by some poisoning in the spinach sandwiches. So there are lots of questions that we want answered How did this happen? *Why did this happen?* What are the family going to do now? There are lots and lots more but who knows the answers?

Charlotte Wallace (12)
The School of St Helen & St Katharine, Oxfordshire

THE DIARY OF JESSICA

Dear Diary,

I haven't made an entry for ages but so much has been happening to me lately, though I'm not quite sure what is to come of it. One thing for sure, I'm finally getting out of this orphanage that has been my home for the last year or so, away from all the annoying little kids who think that playing with babies is interesting, but no one will believe where I'm going to, I'm sure and can only just believe it myself. Mr and Mrs Fossill are adopting me. Michael and Camilla Fossill. My new dad is a footballer and my new mum is a model! I can't believe it! How did this all come about, though?

It was about four weeks ago now and we were on our annual trip to the seaside. It was the best trip though because we went with another orphanage group so there were some people of the same age there. I think Miss Corwell, my teacher, asked this orphanage group along so it would be more interesting for me! We did all the usual things like taking the children across the harbour in a boat etcetera, etcetera. Miss Corwell was really nice and arranged for me and Heather, Tess and Lorna to go to this water slide place. The slides were really cool! My personal favourite was the Thunder Plunger, which was a straight drop down for ten feet in the dark.

I shall have to finish this story later as I can hear my name being called. I probably need to do something with the children, oh well.

Jess.

Dear Diary,

I have some update on my move. I will move in two weeks and they're taking me out to Alton Towers tomorrow. I know that there will be a small part of me that won't want to leave but most of me will be very excited. I still haven't written down how this came to be so . . .

It was one of those horrible grey days and we were down on the beach. I was standing on the rocks by the pier, gazing aimlessly out into the angry sea. I suddenly heard an ear-piercing scream and a splash I saw a young boy in front of me and, without thinking, I jumped in after him and swam towards him. I struggled against the tide and, when I got to him, that was the time when the cold of the sea wrapped round me. My legs went numb but I tried to keep going. I managed to grab hold of him and get his head above the water. The coldness of the sea had gone away, but it felt like it had taken my whole body with it. I swam towards the rocks with him and a man grabbed hold of him and pulled him out of the raging seas to safety. His hands reached out for me, but before I could grab hold, the tide whipped me away. I clung to the rocks, trying hard to keep conscious, my clothes weighing me down, but in vain. I don't remember anything else and when I woke up, I was in a hospital bed. I barely had time to take it all in before the nurse came rushing over to me.

I was soon out of hospital and back at home. A woman came to see Miss Corwell and I was told she was interested in adopting me. She was the mother of the boy whose life I had saved. She wanted to reward me and, when she found out I had no real family, adoption came into her mind. She was Mrs Fossil and I had saved the life of Taylor Fossill and, though he was still unwell, I was assured that he was going to be fine.

I can't wait to go to Alton Towers with them tomorrow. They've taken me out some other times too, so I'm getting to know them really well before the move. They're really nice and I think the adoption will be really successful. (I hope so anyway.)

Jess.

Dear Diary,

I've been a week in my new home and it is great! It's really big too. It has eight bedrooms and the garden is thirty acres. They have also got two tennis courts and an indoor swimming pool. Taylor is a fantastic brother and soon I'm going to have a new baby brother or sister. I'm positive I'm going to be really happy here with my new family and my new life.

Jess.

Elizabeth Sharp (12)
The School of St Helen & St Katharine, Oxfordshire

WEDNESDAY 14TH SEPTEMBER 1911 COLD, WINDY AND SLIGHTLY MISTY. A VICTORIOUS DAY FOR WOMEN

Dear Diary

Cor! What a day. I hope I can fit this in, otherwise I shall have to save all my pennies and shillings to buy another diary, but I don't think it will come to that.

This morning I joined my fellow female pals to march for women's rights, our proposal for the vote tucked under Mrs Pankhurst's arm. Boy, I admire that woman. Of course, we had to make ourselves scarce until it was time, but when the time did eventually come, we were ready in full swing to make a stand! I have to say, it must have been a ruddy good shock for those political blokes, sitting in their big chairs doing all that shouting malarkey.

I can't say I didn't get involved doing the march and all, but I must make it straight that I did not have a thing to do with the violence. Not like that idiotic woman, Martha, I think her name was. Mind you, it gave Mrs Pankhurst enough time to try and bombard the doors. Didn't work though, some of our best were taken by cops, struggling of course, taken into custody I 'eard.

At this point Mrs Pankhurst told us what the situation was. Not good. the politicians had refused to see us and police were starting to pull down banners and placards like a street sweeper sweeping up rubbish and dumping it in the bin. We were still determined to do something, so while back up was sent for we linked as one and forced our way forth. After that we started to make ourselves scarce. I got bitten by one of the reinforcement horses. Peter brought me home, kind he was, seems a bit keen, though. Oh well, that was a great day for women, wasn't it?

See ya,

Emily.

Hannah Forsyth (12)
The School of St Helen & St Katharine, Oxfordshire

WOULD YOU O'DARE TO DO IT?

Many of us will have heard of Red Adair, firefighter international, but fewer of us will know of his Irish counterpart, Murphy O'Dare, who got his name in the paper this week, after he and his colleagues bravely saved the Arabian oil industry.

Early last month an oil well in Saudi Arabia exploded, causing a huge, uncontrollable desert fire.

The manager was in despair. Many of his employees were running to and fro with glasses of water, until one of them became calm and had the bright idea to ring Red Adair, only to find that he had gone on a cruise with his wife to the Caribbean and wouldn't be returning for some time. In yet more anguish, the staff of the aforementioned oil well were frantically flicking through the phone book when they came across Mr M O'Dare's slightly Neanderthal advert:

Me need work quick. Will pose, do errands and fight fires. Ring, etc.

At 5.00 two days after the blaze had begun an Eire Air plane arrived carrying the expected people. Five Irishmen shot out of the plane in a white van, carrying spades. They drove straight past the welcoming party and into the centre of the inferno.

Until a few days ago, they were expected to be dead, when suddenly the fire decreased in size, slowly it began to die down. This of course baffled the Saudi citizens. The fire didn't fully go out until three days ago, when all that was left were five men shovelling sand onto the last spark.

A great ceremony took place yesterday, in which the town's new hero and his cronies were awarded over 3000 Saudi riyals each. It also included a feast and a speech from the mayor.

Today we caught up with Mr O'Dare and asked him what he was going to do with his new-found riches. 'Well, the first ting I'm going to do is get the brakes fixed on my stupid van'. So it was not bravery that drew Murphy O'Dare to the fire but the van in which he travelled.

Daniella Welch (11)
The School of St Helen & St Katharine, Oxfordshire

THE JUDGEMENT OF PARIS

I was grazing my sheep on the luscious pastures of Mount Ida. It was pleasantly sunny, when suddenly the sky darkened and two lofty clouds parted to reveal a window leading directly to Heaven, shrouded in an unearthly aura. From it descended a radiant goddess and I shall do my best to describe her. She was tall and sedate with bewitching, dark eyes, furrowed by two Norman arch eyebrows. She had a prominent jawline and two pronounced cheekbones, giving way to soft, inwardly warped cheeks which seemed equally ready to blaze with passion or pale with malice. Though she was stunning, she had an oppressive presence, like a brewing thunder cloud and an unflinching, patronising gaze, which frosted my veins and chilled my blood. This was Hera, queen of the gods.

Next came a majestic athlete bearing healthy olive skin that contrasted with Hera's ornamental porcelain hue. This goddess was slim, taut and muscular and as her danger-flirting, war hungry, turquoise eyes caught the sunlight, they gave her a bizarre air of aloofness. Though she adorned herself in polished bronze armour with a magnificent breastplate and shield design, underneath she wore the splendid finery of an illustrious Greek gentlewoman. The elaborate satin garment rippled fashionably around the shoulder and fastened there with a bulky jewel-embossed brooch. As the morning sunlight from the east glinted onto it, I saw it was an owl whose emerald eyes glittered mystifying inspiration. It was only when she gently lilted to Earth, did I discover her identity: the marvellous armour, her strength, the brooch and her air of subtle intelligence, it was indeed the goddess of war and wisdom, Athena.

Last of all, floating from the heavenly porthole came what looked like a goddess-sized nymph, as her beauty was so classically womanly. She was dressed just as elegantly as her peers, but in a more typically feminine style with cascading robes, not quite a distinctive hue, but almost one colour and nearly another, reflecting her tantalising nature. She had huge and enchanting eyes, an absorbing violet, whose batting lashes swept over them and flirtatiously raised eyebrows. She had cherry-like, full-cheeks and smooth, lineless temples. Below her pert, petal-like nose were her garnet-red, voluptuous lips. Her waterfall of treacle curls meandered down her slender, bare back as she cooed meekly, 'Paris, Paris, don't fall to your knees praising us,' she paused to flick her hair suggestively, 'for it is we who must mimic your beseeching pose as we must ask of you a favour.'

Instantly I knew that this glorious apparition was the lovely Aphrodite, the illustration of animalistic desires and lust of all mankind. She smiled coyly and gestured with grace to her companion, Athena. The goddess of victory retrieved from behind her a glistening golden apple inscribed with the phrase, *For the fairest woman in the world.* 'Listen,' she said, fixing her searingly inspirational eyes on me so that I was compelled to do her bidding. 'We have lately attended the wedding of Peleus and Thetis. All those worthy in the world and the entire company of Olympus were invited - except for that troublesome fiendess of quarrels and strife - Eris. In retaliation for this insult, her livid temper raged and she hurled into the proceedings this apple. The winner of the trophy, of course, fitting the inscription. We have disputed and disputed, but,' she smiled wryly, 'we simply cannot come to an agreement.'

'So, mortal, prove your worth as an impartial judge and announce the fairest! As high queen of Earth and Heaven, I pronounce you ruler of all the eye beholds from this mountain's zenith,' coaxed Hera with treacle sweetness, then batted her eyelids vindictively, 'but you must choose me.'

'Is it not far more rewarding to know that you have earned your prosperity through courage and military strategy?' Athena offered, and then a little more sternly, 'But the apple must be mine.' I turned to Aphrodite in order to consider the final reward.

'Oh, gracious lady,' I bowed in reverence, 'What is your offer, oh divine temptress?'

'Oh sweet, sweet boy, tell me, what is intelligence and wealth, when every man is surely lost without a good woman at his side and to you I offer the most tender Helen of Sparta.'

'Aphrodite, oh goddess of devilish wantonness, the apple is yours if Helen be mine.'

She received the apple with a winning smile and stared in mocking triumph at her rivals who smouldered with jealousy and gradually faded away.

Hannah Wilson (12)
The School of St Helen & St Katharine, Oxfordshire

DREAMS OF AFRICA

From the rising of dawn to the setting of dusk, those were the hours in which we, black slaves, are forced to work and serve the 'egotistical' whites. As the day ends, exhausted and hungry, we are rounded up and sent back through the dark to our old, weathered, small and smelly shack. There, tiredness seeps over our over-worked and ill-treated minds, as we lie down on the old wooden floor, with the mice and rats amongst us and a moth-bitten blanket between us. Every night I can remember I have had a dream playing inside my mind. It begins dark . . .

I am up in the air, flying over the deserted plains and cramped, poor villages of Africa. Darkness surrounds me squeezing out all my happy feelings and leaving me bare. Then, as I doze off inside my dream, screams arise, making every little hair on my body stand on end, pricking my skin with fear. I then see fire and injustice raid my world. The powerful whites tread down the black villagers and enslave them. They split families apart and never once think about the blacks' feelings and make money out of selling my people's lives. Pain and hatred fill the land with despair, leaving the dominant whites to kill and rule our suffering lives.

I can see a thick and dangerous line being drawn between the rich and poor, black and white, causing injustice among the natives. Evil creeps over the good, like armies of ants and storms of locusts destroying the peace and love there once was. As the disaster reaches its peak below me, I start falling. Always at this point, I try to pull my eyes apart and wake up, before any other horrors inside my head are revealed, but as I scream, dawn breaks.

Birds begin singing as the sun, shining in full glory and wealth, peeps its warmth and light over the horizon. I know I am smiling, colour wars have ended and ahead of me is good and prosperity. I can see a blue sky fringed with white fluffy clouds and flocks of birds chirp overhead. I pass fields of green and red flowers and white, sculpted cliffs tower over the clean, clear water of a lagoon.

It is as if I am flying over a new, changed Africa, full of wealth where colours and backgrounds do not seem to matter. I see happy clusters of round hut villages, girls and boys, black and white, playing and laughing as one big family. Everyone has left the past behind them, forgiven and forgotten. Even I feel different and somehow free, free as in free to go anywhere and everywhere, free to live and choose, free to be happy and treat others how you would like to be treated. I feel new and somewhat changed, even a different person altogether leading a different life, the way I want to live. I am able to be educated, and get decently paid jobs and even have a family.

I look down on mothers washing by the riverside, nearby fathers tending the cattle herds. I see freedom, peace and happiness stretched ahead of me. I seem to be closing in on a family, as I get closer I see it's my family. There is my mama and my baby brother, Ali. She looks up at me and smiles. Her big brown eyes sparkle and glint in the sunshine and Ali gurgles his joy. Smiling, I touch the ground, nothing between me and her and we run together and hug for the first time in my seven years of enslavement. With no one to stop me and yell at me to go back to work, I am free to hug her the rest of my days but someone approaches. I'm sure he is familiar and then it clicks. Papa, my papa. He runs forward and joins the hug. When at last we break free, he lifts me up and places me on his strong and muscular shoulders. I laugh for I am smothered in happiness and tears of joy enter my eyes.

Always at this moment, as I once again touch the mud ground, the picture fades and I am nudged vigorously and yelled at to wake up. However, when I do, I always feel golden and special, which keeps me going all the way through the next laborious day. I tell myself at the moment, while I am young, that what I have just dreamt is only just a dream, but one day when I am free from enslavement I shall, although there will be risks, make my Dream of Africa a reality.

Fiona Rushbrook (12)
The School of St Helen & St Katharine, Oxfordshire

HOLIDAY HORROR

Every year we go on holiday to the same place; Mum, Dad, my younger
brother Chris and I. We stay in the same bungalow in the same village,
in the same dreary country (England) and we go to the same beach. We
do exactly the same things we did when we were little. I used to love it,
but for the last couple of years it had got boring. Very boring. There are
never any girls my age to hang around with, so I end up playing football
with Chris. This year was very different though . . .

For once, the weather was very hot, and there was a family in the
bungalow next door, instead of the senile old folk that are usually there.
The Logan family didn't arrive until the day after us. I was in the
garden, fetching the wet swimming things from the line when I heard a
voice.
'Hello, you must be about Vic's age,' I squinted into the sun.
'I'm thirteen next September,' I replied.
'Great, and is that your brother I saw out the front?'
'Yup, that's Chris.'
'Well, he's about the same age as Jamie. That's cool!'
'Sorry, I have to go now,' I said. I felt annoyed. Why do adults always
think you will get on with other people, just because you are the same
age?

Later on, at the beach when I was reading a magazine that I had bought
from Woolies, a girl came up to me.
'Hi!' she said, 'I'm Victoria.' She was thin, with cat-like eyes. 'You can
call me Vic though. Come on, come and have some fun.' She took the
magazine out of my arms, 'Trust me, it'll be a laugh!' Vic dragged me
down to the shore.

I just dipped my toes in, imperturbably, but Vic dived into each wave,
and started swimming perfect butterfly, very far out. I watched, until
she swam back.
'You're an excellent swimmer!' I exclaimed, rather jealously. 'I can
only swim a width of our local pool.'
'Dad taught me. He can teach you if you like.'

Frank Logan said he would be happy to teach me, and by the end of the week, I could swim breaststroke, and nearly front crawl.

One morning, after breakfast, when I was reluctantly washing up the dirty dishes, Vic came round. She had a tear-stained face. She said to me, 'My Grandma has severe cancer. We have to go home, because the doctor says she doesn't have long to live.' She scribbled something down on a piece of paper. 'Here, this is my address, write to me!' She hurriedly thrust it into my hands and ran off down the path.

On the last day of our holiday, Mum told us to stay out of her way because she was busy packing and didn't want to be disturbed. I wanted to go to the sea, to practise my swimming one last time, but I knew she wouldn't let me go in a million years, so I left a note. *Dear Mum and Dad, gone to Carswell Bay to swim. Back soon, Heather.*

I got out my towel and swimsuit, and headed off towards the beach. The water was freezing, but once I was in, I was fine. As usual I swam breaststroke along the shore. It was quite hard though, because there were so many kids mucking about.

Then suddenly, to my great surprise, Vic popped out of the water.
'Vic, you're back!' I gasped. She looked somehow different, her skin was silvery and her general appearance was wraithlike.
'Yeah, hi. Shall we swim out further? It's too crowded around here.'
Vic swam out, but saw me hesitating, so she yelled, 'Come on, you big baby!'
I don't like to be called a baby, so I was impassive, and followed her, but soon I was out of my depth. I looked back towards the shore, but it was a long way off. I called to Vic, but her eyes glittered spitefully.
'You're out of depth, aren't you!' she sneered. Scared, I looked back towards the shore, but her voice followed me.
'You can't go back now!' she snapped, 'the current is too strong, and you are too weak.'
I felt panic welling up inside me. I started to choke. I tried to kick, but I had no energy left. Suddenly, I felt strong hands grasp me around the middle and before I knew it, I felt sand on my back. I tried to stand up, but I just collapsed. I heard a man's voice shouting, then I was carried across the beach to somewhere less crowded. I coughed up a lot of salty sea water, then opened my eyes. Dad was standing there, looking both a

mixture of cross and concerned. Then the lifeguard spoke, 'I would get her home and dry, Sir. I think she's learnt her lesson!'

Later that day, I sent a letter to Vic, asking why she had wanted to hurt me. A week later, I received a letter from Mrs Logan, reading,

Dear Heather,
I know this will come as a shock to you, but I'm afraid Victoria had a horrible accident the day we arrived back home. She was on her bike, and unfortunately collided with a motorbike and died on the way to hospital. Thank you for making her last holiday a happy one.
Yours, Jules Logan
Victoria's mother.

Rebecca Green (12)
The School of St Helen & St Katharine, Oxfordshire

WIMBLEDON WINNER

Serena Williams, the women's tennis no 2 beat her sister, Venus Williams in the Wimbledon Ladies' tennis championships for the first time yesterday.

This is the second time that two sisters have had to play each other in the Wimbledon Grand Slam final, the first was in 1884 when Maud Watson beat her sister Lilian Watson.

It was a close match given that the two tennis champions, who are great friends, were playing each other. In the first set Serena broke Venus' serve twice putting her in the lead by several games. For quite a long time Venus was two or three games behind Serena and it looked as if there was no hope for the twenty-two-year-old. However, the winner of Wimbledon 2000 and 2001, wouldn't let her younger sister get away that fast because soon after she broke back, evening the score. After a lot of breaking, smash shots and aces the two American athletes had to play a tiebreak because the score was six games each. Serena's powerful strokes helped her win the first set. In the second set Venus broke Serena's serve, putting herself in the lead, but the twenty-year-old Serena evened the score just as her sister had done in the first set. The game was extremely tight; the mother of Serena and Venus didn't clap in case she made it appear that she wanted one of her daughters to win. She sat there with a straight face watching contentedly as the two champions battled it out for the top trophy in tennis.

Apart from making tennis history, this match is truly one to remember.

Rebecca Stewart (12)
The School of St Helen & St Katharine, Oxfordshire

HOW TO SPOT GHOSTS

It is said that when a ghost kills a person, the ghost becomes a person, and the person becomes a ghost.

Four girls went camping alone out in the woods with a book called 'How to Spot Ghosts'. The girls were so excited about going camping in the woods alone, they had brought marshmallows to toast on a campfire. It took them a long time, but finally they pitched their tent. They easily made a campfire as they had brought a lighter with them. They cooked baked beans and Cara started singing, 'Beans, beans good for your heart, the more you eat the more you . . .' but she was laughing by the end. After having a meal of baked beans on bread, they toasted marshmallows over their campfire.

It was a cold and icy night in the middle of winter, but for some reason the girls were extremely hot, wearing shorts and T-shirts. They were happily singing songs around the campfire and having loads of fun, giggling and telling jokes, when Leah suggested they read their book on how to spot ghosts. Lizzie went and got the book; she started reading it aloud, 'It is said that when a ghost kills a person, the ghost becomes a person, and the person becomes a ghost.'
The girls were scared, but intrigued to find out more.
'You can tell when a ghost is around because the surroundings are ice cold, yet you feel boiling hot,' continued Cara.
The girls looked at each other . They felt incredibly hot even though it was late in a midwinter night, but they all tried to persuade each other they were hot because of the hard work in putting up the tent. Pretending to be brave, Emily continued, 'When a ghost is nearby, you can hear nothing but people's voices.'
The girls were silent, so was the night. They could not hear wind but could see the tree branches moving. They could not hear owls hooting, but could see their beaks moving. They could hear nothing, not even their campfire crackling. The girls were at this stage terrified, but Leah continued, 'You can see tiny little flies glowing in the shape of the ghost's victim.'
The girls looked around then each screamed when one by one they saw tiny flies in the shape of themselves.

The girls petrified ran into their tent, hoping, praying that it was a coincidence and they were imagining things. They were so scared they could hardly breathe. First Cara strangled. Next Lizzie suffocated. Then Emily stabbed. Last Leah, hung from a tall pine tree. The ghosts were no longer ghosts, they were the same people they used to be fifty years ago, Rodney Anderson, Harold Smith, Claire Palm and Jessica Harris. They all ran off happily shrieking, so joyful they were people again. The girls were no longer girls though. They were ghosts.

It is said that when a ghost kills a person, the ghost becomes a person, and the person becomes a ghost.

Suzanne Russell (13)
The School of St Helen & St Katharine, Oxfordshire

OLD MAJOR HAD A DREAM

Mr Jones and his men of Manor Farm, or should I say 'Animal Farm', have been kicked out by, you'll never guess, the animals themselves. It all started when 'Old Major', as the animals liked to call him, had a dream. His dream was about a rebellion and how unfair life was on the farm and, if man was not there, then the animals would be better off without him.

Old Major died three days after his dream and so the two pigs, Napoleon and Snowball, took charge of this rebellion. We asked Snowball why the animals chose to rebel just before harvest. This is what Snowball said, 'We had to rebel as soon as we could really, no matter what stood in our way. We rebelled because Mr Jones was not feeding us and we would be able to do the harvest quicker than he did anyway, and we did, even the ducks helped!'

After Mr Jones had been kicked out, the animals painted *Animal Farm* on the gate instead of *Manor Farm*. They also wrote up seven commandments on the wall of the house:
1. Whatever goes upon two legs is an enemy.
2. Whatever goes upon four legs, or has wings, is a friend.
3. No animal shall wear clothes.
4. No animal shall sleep in a bed.
5. No animal shall drink alcohol.
6. No animal shall kill any other animal.
7. All animals are equal.

When asked why the animals rebelled, Boxer replied, 'We didn't have much choice. This is what Old Major wanted and so we felt it was our job to do what he asked. We also rebelled as we were being so badly treated; we were getting whipped and as Snowball said we just weren't getting fed. I think Mr Jones just forgot to feed us. When we got rid of Mr Jones we burnt the whips and lots of other nasty things too!'

So that tells us about Old Major's dream and how the animals carried out, but just remember, animals can be more powerful than you think!

Emma Williams (13)
The School of St Helen & St Katharine, Oxfordshire

AUTUMN LEAVES

Autumn got onto the plane with tears rolling down her cheeks like leaves falling from a tree. She gazed out of the window to see her sister Rosie waving goodbye. Autumn was going to miss England so much, but knew that she had to move on. Her husband had died fighting in the war a few years ago and if she wanted to forget him then she had to leave. Rosie had been so good to her, letting her stay with her. Autumn even had a good job which she loved. There was a bit of her that didn't want to go as she backtracked her memories.

Suddenly the plane elevated into the air. Autumn's heart was pounding like the beating of drums as she looked down at her sister. She forced a smile through her tears as she waved a goodbye with her shaking hand. The plane rose higher into the air. Autumn settled back in her seat knowing that she had made the right decision. She took a deep breath and looked ahead to her life in America.

Baleni Balachandran (13)
Wallington High School For Girls, Surrey

SUMMER

The sun is high in the clear blue sky, with light, fluffy clouds all around. The turquoise sea makes a gentle slooshing sound, as it meets the sandy yellow shore. The beach is crowded with hundreds of people. They all have their windbreaks up and picnic rugs out. Children sit on the sand building sandcastles, while others squeal when their tiny, wriggling toes meet the icy water.

Up on the sand dunes a fresh smell of ice cream mixes with the warm aroma of burgers, sizzling on a barbecue. A huge, long line of hot sweaty people, kids and adults, queue to devour their long-awaited ice creams. Everyone with an ice cream already has a broad smile across their face because they are now a lot cooler than before.

Suddenly a small girl screams with delight as she sees a tiny mud crab scuttle past her small, sandy feet. She follows it all the way to a picturesque rock pool that is filled with all sorts of other beautiful creatures. The chubby-cheeked child gently picks up a pearly white shell, glistening in the sunlight. She pulls back the murky green seaweed and tosses it in the water, to reveal the rest of the dainty shell.

Jane Wilkin (13)
Wallington High School For Girls, Surrey

THE LAST ONE STANDING

Stretching and sitting quietly is the way I prepare myself for an audition for ballet, mentally and physically. To warm up my feet I hold onto the wall and rise slowly onto pointe. To start off with it felt like pins were sticking into my feet, but as time went on the pain died down a little.

A lady walked through the door which was terracotta and called us to the stage. She was short and had a strange voice, which reminded me of an owl, that was waking up at the beginning of night, loud and wide-awake with large glowing eyes. She then lined us up into number order and told us to follow her onto the platform, which would later be developed into a stage. As soon as I walked in from the wings at the side of the stage, the bright light hit my eyes like the sunlight through a curtain, and the beam was staring right at me. I started to walk into my line, while my legs were getting more and more like jelly. I then waited for the audition but I knew I had to shake myself together otherwise I wouldn't be able to dance my best.

The audition was two hours and I felt like a lion wanting to escape, but no longer having the energy too. Finally it was over and I could sit down and wait for my call to see whether I could be in the 'Nutcracker Show' or not. As the owl lady stood up and started her speech I could feel my stomach producing more and more butterflies every second. She started calling out the numbers who would be in the show, 32, 38, 40, 42 . . . 45. I was in! I leapt up and a huge flush of relief escaped my body and I felt like a butterfly that had just escaped its cocoon. I hoped that I would always be the 'last one standing'.

Katie Timothy (13)
Wallington High School For Girls, Surrey

A DAY IN THE LIFE OF AN ELEPHANT

Each day, I wake up from my wonderful dreams of freedom and happiness, just to find myself in a cramped, foul smelling, enclosed space; in a cage.

Every morning, I wonder why I am here; or why a creature like me should ever deserve to live in this dirty, dismal, confined place. What I need is my habitat, so I can gallop freely whenever I like, so I can lie in green pastures all day, so I can soak myself in rivers of cool, refreshing, pure water, with no one to stop me. But what I need most is love. No animal can live without love.

Slowly, I plod towards my food trough, only to find remnants of muddy food, which tastes awful. Nevertheless, this is the only nourishment available, so I must eat it. The stale flavours of old potato peel and sour apple skin spreads through my mouth, creating a queasy feeling in my empty stomach.

At this point, wide-eyed children and beady-eyed adults stare nosily through my cage. Why anyone would ever dream to watch the dull, slow life of an elephant like me is a complete wonder? However, this irritates me deeply: I am entitled to my privacy.

By now, I feel tired out by boredom, and I begin to dream of my life as a young elephant in those everlasting meadows brimming with wildlife, and of my family who loved me more than the world. And once again, I am reunited with them in my sleep.

Judith Tang (13)
Wallington High School For Girls, Surrey

THE DREAMTIME

In the beginning the Earth was dark and bare. Guthi-Guthi, the spirit of our ancestral being, who lived in the sky came down and wanted to create a special land for people and animals, so he set borders.

Guthi-Guthi set one foot on Gunderbooka Mountain and the other foot on Mount Grenfell. He looked at the bare land and wanted water and plants, but he knew that the water serpent was trapped inside Mount Minara, called Weowie. He called out to the serpent, 'Weowie, Weowie!' but Weowie couldn't hear because he was trapped in the mountain, so Guthi-Guthi rose up into the sky, and called out again, but still, Weowie did not react, so Guthi-Guthi came down and roared as loud as thunder, and banged on the mountain so hard that it split open. Then Weowie came out and made waterholes, and streams in the land, travelling all over the land. Later Weowie went back to his home in the mountain.

Guthi-Guthi wanted more water in the land, hence he called upon Old Pundu, the cod. Therefore it was his duty to drag, and crate the Darling River. Thus the cod came out with Mudlark, his little companion, and they set off, up in the north, and created the huge river. And even now the river flows right down our country, Australia.

This country was formed, and so were the first two tribes. They were called Eaglehawk and Crow. All other tribes came from these two tribes.

Gabriela Raison (13)
Wallington High School For Girls, Surrey

A DAY IN THE LIFE OF THE MAN ON THE MOON

Everybody thinks that I'm completely crazy wanting to live on the moon. My name is Craig Crater and I reckon the moon is a great place to stay. All the hustle and bustle of the city is gone and it is a paradise of peace and harmony.

Many people say it must be lonely and boring without any company or games but I can have lots of fun when I want to, like when people who think I'm a myth walk through the night and look up to see me perched on the edge of a crater smiling down and waving at them. Once the bewildered face of an eight-year-old boy made me laugh so much I nearly fell off the moon and plummeted down to Earth. The child's pupils were the size of bowling balls, but in his eye there was a certain glint of excitement. However, his chubby, cheeky little face was as white as a sheet and his jaw had dropped about ten feet lower than its normal position. It was hilarious!

I'm going to eat dinner now. I think I'll have Edam cheese from the east side of the moon today. Although, my favourites are Brie cheese and Swiss cheese from the south and west of my home.

I'll see you soon - bye!

Emily King (13)
Wallington High School For Girls, Surrey

A Day In The Life Of . . .

At the beginning of my day I feel like a bird soaring above the trees, wild and free without a care in the world. Gliding around, swooping down low, twisting and twirling to my heart's content.

Then come the people. Little old grannies scared witless, their knobbly knees shaking as they glide through the sky and dive to the ground narrowly missing the Earth. Teenage boys shouting to friends, 'I'm not afraid, are you?' Full of bravado, then clinging on for dear life, terrified out of their wits, but of course they deny it as soon as they depart.

The ones I detest the most are snotty little kids grappling with me and shrieking with joy. Oh how I wish I could let them go and watch them plummet to the Earth. But today was worse! I was squished and squashed with a pain in my stomach as a massive man tried to squeeze in. I felt like a lark trapped in a cage with no space to spread my wings, but luckily my arms wouldn't fit around his middle to lock him in safely, so he was made to leave and a tiny girl was placed there instead. She was so light and free she made me feel as if there was no one there at all!

Bidding farewell to the hoards, I welcome my night without motion until, the gates of the theme park open once more.

Gabrielle Cooper (13)
Wallington High School For Girls, Surrey

A WALK IN A SPANISH STREET

A step outside of the cool, air-conditioned hotel sends strands of hair brushing against your neck, as the fan above the doors sweep your curls behind you. The automated doors close, the warm air welcomes you outdoors and the sun shines brightly on the grey, concrete pavement.

Walking along the pavement beside the beach, you enter a noisy arcade with machines that only work with the insertion of money. You are enticed into a Spanish sweet shop, a fresh-smelling fruit stall, and follow the warm, 'just baked' bread aroma to the bakery. After satisfying your hungry, grumbling stomach you carry on down the pavement and buy a delicious double-scoop ice cream on a crispy cone. You get shivers down your spine as the cold ice cream touches your teeth and melts in your humid mouth.

With your shoes off you walk on the sandy beach, the golden sand feels warm on the soles of your feet. Wriggling your toes deeper into the sand, it feels relaxingly cooler.

The sea is a clear glittery blue, sparkling in the sunlight like flawless diamonds. You watch the waves wet the sand, as they ebb and tide; you hear the seagulls and spot a few bobbing up and down on the water's surface.

As day sneakily evaporates, the sun begins setting and darkness gradually envelops. The sky looks radiant like a fire, as it gradates from a rich, warm red, orange, yellow to a dark, mysterious blue. The towering palm trees gently sway in the calm breeze.

Meryljo Ching (13)
Wallington High School For Girls, Surrey

SURVIVOR

It was a bitterly cold day and the snowstorm outside was like a swirling wall of ice. No one ventured out in it, no one but Sky, a young girl of thirteen who had wandered off from her family with her dog, Star. She had found shelter in a cave away from the storm but the howling wind still sent shivers up her spine. Sky had attempted to light a fire but had failed. Star whined in the corner, too hungry and too cold to sleep.

Sky and Star had been through a lot together as they had been in this wilderness for three months already. Her first test for survival was a fight with a bear which fortunately she won. It had been almost two months ago on a day like this that she had walked into this very cave and found it inhabited with a grizzly bear. She and Star had fought it with only their bare hands and a rock. Star attacked the lower body whilst Sky had mustered all her strength to throw the rock onto the creature's head.

There had been a tremendous crack when she finally struck it and the bear fell heavily to the ground narrowly missing Star. They had come back to this cave ever since. They ate the bear with melted snow and skinned it and used the fur for clothes . . .

Jessica Trimnell (13)
Wallington High School For Girls, Surrey

RUNNING FREE

I didn't know what to do next. I was in the cubicle now. Should I risk running out of the cubicle or stay in here forever? I tried to stand up on a little ledge in the cubicle but that didn't work. My sweating hands scraped down the mirror and left marks on it. I tried again, struggling and clambering up the walls. I didn't know what else to do. My hands slid down the hard cold walls. Every movement took a lifetime and an enormous effort. I was putting my heart and soul into climbing up the walls. I tried to hold on as best as I could, but my arms weren't having any of that. They were too weak and too tired, so were my legs. I was sliding down the walls. I tried to grip on with my worn out trainers but the grip on them wasn't good enough. Then I fell. Scraping my knees and elbows on the walls once again, hitting the stone-cold, cheap carpet covered the floors like a tonne of bricks. It was like I was falling through time. I was spinning, twisting, turning and tumbling all at the same time. Then I stopped. The last thing I felt was the uncomfortable feeling of the scratchy carpet and my very sore arms and legs.

Then I heard a voice. It was quite deep and it had a certain strangeness about it. I couldn't see who it was because my eyes were filled with tears. I screamed thinking it was him. 'Go away! Leave me alone!' I was now shouting at the top of my voice. 'Why are you chasing me?'
'It's okay love.' It was a different voice this time. A more caring, kind voice.
'Where am I? Get him away from me!' I was still screaming and my voice was starting to get sore from where I had been screaming so much. Then I thought of all of the people in the shop staring at me like I was a little kid screaming because they can't have the sweets that they wanted. I felt embarrassed. I was beginning to turn into a spoilt brat. I hated myself.

I started to try and get up. I stumbled a little, wiped back my tears and made my way out of the changing room area. I tasted blood on my tongue; I must have cut my lip as I fell. My knees were dragging me down to the floor with every step. I couldn't carry on any longer. I tried to run out of the shop but all I ended up doing was lying sprawled out over the floor in the middle of the shop. I couldn't believe what I had nearly done. I was about to run out of the shop; ignorant to him who was chasing me only minutes before.

I got up again. This time I actually got out of the shop. I knew I looked a mess, but I didn't care. All I wanted to do right now was get home before anything else could happen. I started to walk faster but it wasn't long before I couldn't face the shame of seeing anyone so I ran. I ran faster and faster, letting all my cares disappear with every step of the way. I was free at last.

Jennifer Casey (13)
Wallington High School For Girls, Surrey

FROGS, DOGS AND BIG, BIG TROUBLE

21st May 2002 - 10am

I don't want to be a teenager. Teenagers are always moody and get loads of homework and worst of all they *kiss* boys! Ugh!

I'm only 9, so I don't get moody (much) and my teacher, Miss Thomas, is considerate and doesn't give us homework. Most importantly though, I *hate* boys! They're always muddy and like playing pointless games like football.
Girls are clean and like dolls and normal things like . . . frogs.

5pm

Mum says I have to wash my hair now. That's so unfair. It's not that greasy, I only washed it last week.

6pm

I'm going to Louise's party now. I've got my high heels on. Sally's not allowed heels like mine, because her mum says they will ruin her feet. Sally's mum's a fibber though because my feet are perfectly normal.

22nd May 2002 - 3pm

Mum has made me let all my animals and insects out of their jars. Can't she see that they need me to look after them! She told me it's cruel to animals but I can see through her, she's scared of them. Wimp!

5:30pm

I've got Freddie, my frog, in a box under my bed.

6pm

Oh dear! Mum's furious. She found Freddie hopping around her room. How was I to know he wouldn't stay in his box? She thinks he's dirty, but he isn't because I gave him a wash in the sink earlier.

26th May 2002 - 4pm

Yuck! Beans and broccoli. Well I'm not eating them.

4:05pm

I've eaten them; Mum said there'd be no pudding if I didn't. That's bluemail that is.

4:06pm

I mean blackmail.

28th May 2002 - 11am

At my dad's house.
I much prefer Mum to his new girlfriend, Stephanie, they didn't use to kiss all the time. Yuck! I'd hate to get all wet like that, I'd rather just shake hands.

29th May 2002 - 4:30pm

At my friend Sally's house, we're playing Animal Hospital with her dog, Charlie.

5pm

Mum came to pick me up early, because Sally's mum asked her to. Apparently Charlie doesn't need his hair cut! Sally and me thought he did.

6:30pm

In bed at 6:30pm for a whole week just for cutting a dog's hair. It's not fair! I can't wait to be a teenager; you can stay up as late as you want!

Cara Winter (13)
Wallington High School For Girls, Surrey

A DAY IN THE LIFE OF A CATERPILLAR

As I peeked through the gaps in my eyes, the sun's rays entered like children being let into a playground after a stressful school day. I wondered for a moment what this new day would bring, then I remembered it would just be a typical day; wake up and eat, like every other day. I froze. Right before my tiny feet I saw a plant, it wasn't any ordinary plant, it was a four-leaf clover. My face lit up, a large rush of confidence ran straight through my spine. I had guessed wrong, this day had just started!

I scuttled to the patch of grass I always eat from. To my surprise the grass was even greener. I ate very quickly; I didn't even think I actually had time to chew. I was full, slowly I closed my eyes.

'Where am I!' I whispered. I was surrounded by cloth that was tightly wrapped. I was so uncomfortable. There was nothing I could do, until I found a small exit; I crept through. Suddenly I saw a shadow, it grew closer and closer. It was the foot of a human! I ran as fast as the wind but nothing happened, when to my surprise I gave one big push and wings came out of me. Yes! I had turned into a butterfly. My gracious wings spread out. I had turned into a butterfly. I glided wondering what my wings would lead me to.

Adedoyin Sokan (13)
Wallington High School For Girls, Surrey

GHOSTS

They had gone, but now I wished I wasn't so alone. I was alone because it was just the night and I. I tried to ignore the fear that spread through me like an infectious disease. Gregory had said my house was in a quadrant for the best spiritual behaviour. That meant, my house was a tourist site for ghosts. Luckily, I didn't believe in ghosts. There was no real evidence that proved ghosts existence. Circumstantial evidence, yes. Evidence that proved ghosts existed, no. The sky was rude and arrogant, as if it saw me and decided I wasn't good enough to be its friend. Jumping, turning and twisting. Not being rough, not rough yet, anyway.

My pyjamas smelled strongly of fabric conditioner, a sickly odour. They were warm from being on the radiator, heating my stone-cold body. The bears along the bottom grinned savagely, revealing continuous sets of white teeth. Exiting the room I found the lounge window wide open, strange. Strange because no one had opened the window. Strange because it was closed last time I checked. Strange because the window couldn't have opened by itself, so someone or something must have opened it. The night didn't welcome me. Instead it ignored me showing off its tricks on a skateboard. Howls and criticisms swept past me as I leaned forward clumsily.

Indusha Selvanathar (13)
Wallington High School For Girls, Surrey

THE SANDMAN

Hi, my name's Kat, Kat Knight. This is my story . . .

It all began on a Friday night. I was out clubbing in London with a few mates. My boyfriend was there too, Ollie. It was that night that my luck changed. It was in the early hours of the morning that I caught him kissing another girl. He caught my eye and I gave him the dirtiest look I'd ever given. I quickly turned on my heel and left. He ran after me, but I was having none of it. He gave me those puppy-dog eyes that I fell for when I first met him. Instead of saying something in return, I kept walking. A loud noise, glaring headlights and *bang!* I was dead.

I woke up not in my own bed to find that it had been a bad dream, or even in hospital, I was in a barren wasteland. The land was a sandy-brown and had bits of green grass sprouting out of the ground. There were doors - just doors - dotted around the place. This didn't look like I was in England at all.

As I searched for a familiar face, I realised I wasn't wearing my own clothes any more. I was wearing blue striped pyjamas, fluffy blue slippers and perched on top of my head was a blue nightcap. I turned around in a panic. I felt something hit my chest. I was wearing a silver chain, with a blue plaque attached to it. It read, *The Sandman* . . .

Stacey Palmer (13)
Wallington High School For Girls, Surrey

AFTER DARK

As I stand at the bottom of the steps I know that that time has come again. Clowns are cartwheeling in my stomach. I take one step, my hand gripping tightly to the railing beside me. I know that I must be prepared.

As I reach the last step, my bare feet drowning sweat, but the worst is yet to come. As my hand reaches out for the handle in front of me, I quickly take a glance around, checking if anyone is there, but I might as well be blind. I take a huge breath and I manage to push open the creaking door.

I spy it, where it always is. Instead of walking to it, I run and jump. My silk pyjamas clutching to my skin. As I pull over my duvet I can hear creaks. Tears of fear are coming to my eyes. Please not . . . the monsters are under the bed. I can make out the shadows of the monsters waiting to pounce; I can still hear the monsters under the bed.

I can now hear footsteps, I am paralysed with fear. The door slowly opens and I can hear roaring. Then all becomes clear, the light comes on. My dad is yawning, and the shadows of the monsters, belong to my dressing gown. My dad kisses me goodnight. I point a shaky finger under the bed. He gets down on his hands and knees, but I don't see what he does for I am in dreamland.

Katherine Moore (13)
Wallington High School For Girls, Surrey

THESEUS THWARTED

Yesterday the notorious Theseus went into the labyrinth but never came out.

Theseus a 23-year-old body builder went into the labyrinth to fight the imprisoned Minotaur. The Minotaur, a half man, half bull eats seven men and seven women a day, only yesterday he could have eaten eight men instead.

Theseus had grown close to the King of Crete's daughter, who had given him advice on how to kill the Minotaur and make it back out of the labyrinth without getting lost. She gave him a sword and a piece of string, or so we thought!

When Theseus departed into the labyrinth he didn't know that the string and the sword weren't going to be useful. Theseus was meant to use the string to help him find his way back out of the labyrinth, but when Theseus had been in there five minutes, the King set fire to the string which slowly burnt along, then he pulled the frazzled thread back out of Theseus' hands.

When Theseus met the Minotaur he must have pulled out his sword, which didn't exist. The sword was as big as my little finger and was completely blunt.

It was obviously the King and his daughter who had come up with the dastardly plan.

The King commented, 'Don't trust anyone'.

It has been 24 hours since Theseus was last seen, now he knows not to trust anyone.

Catherine Hollis (13)
Wallington High School For Girls, Surrey

JUST MY IMAGINATION

In this dark, depressing room you can't really see anything. The only way of knowing if something is there is by banging into it, so far I have found two armchairs and a sofa. I'm not sure I want to move here any more but it is too late, my parents have bought it. This room really does stink, like a bedpan that hasn't been changed for months.

It sounds like I'm not the only one in this room, there are quiet, shrill squeaks coming from under the floorboards. Uh! Oh! Mice! My mum hates mice, we will probably have to move again.

I decided to take a seat on the couch, I had a feeling that my parents would be ages with the removal van. As I sat down a lot of dust came up making a grey cloud above my head. My seat felt extremely uncomfortable. It was as solid as gold. I decided to investigate. I flipped over the cushion, I felt some buttons. Just as I was about to undo them, the lights flicked on, my mother came in. 'Mel why didn't you turn on the lights?'
'Sorry, I forgot!' I stammered.

This room is bright when you turn on the lights and you can see everything. The furniture is lovely and comfortable. My parents were chatting with our lovely neighbours and the noises were them talking, not mice.

Sometimes my imagination gets carried away!

Maria Bryan (13)
Wallington High School For Girls, Surrey

ATTACK IN THE SEA!

After twenty minutes on the beach, Mum said that she needed to get some suncream from the hotel, as her shoulders were going red. Dad needed the toilet anyway so he went with Mum, leaving me in charge of Matt, my little brat of a brother.

When Mum and Dad were out of sight, Matt jumped into the sea before I could stop him. I told him not to go in as Mum warned us not to, but he just said Mum was trying to spoil our fun. I didn't make a fuss, as the glistening turquoise water looked calm.

After a while of playing in the water, Matt started screaming. The lifeguard quickly jumped in his motorboat and headed for Matt. As the motorboat got to Matt the lifeguard lifted him out of the water and rushed him to the shore. Matt was screaming in agony, this was no joke. My eyes started pouring with tears, soaking my whole face. People crowded around him and pushed me out of the way. I heard someone say something about a jellyfish sting. This made my heart race. I could just make out that the lifeguard was putting something on Matt's leg.

I saw Mum and Dad come rushing down after seeing the crowd around Matt. The lifeguard said that Matt would be fine but would have to stay in hospital overnight for observation.

The day after, Matt was back and glad to be out of hospital.

Rachel Brewer (13)
Wallington High School For Girls, Surrey

A Day In The Life Of Anne Frank

Dear Kitty,

Today is the most terrible day of my life; everyone is dull and dreary today. Papa is ailing and Mama is very upset, all because of Adolf Hitler, he is evil, a demon and a ferocious menace.

Last night five houses in the little street where we are living were bombed. All that remains is a miniature brown box which lay under slivers of glass, where Mr Crooks once lived.

That is another reason why everyone is upset because Mr Crooks has sadly passed away.

As I heard the strident bombs go off I was very positive that we were going to die, however Mama is trying to assure me that we will survive by saying, 'We should think good, blissful, lovely thoughts.' Everything Mama says never seems to make a difference. No matter how much I try I know that we are all going to die dreadfully soon.

If I've told you once, I've told you a thousand times that the little room where we are hiding is repulsive, malodorous and hideous, it will never be like home. I brought some posters of my much loved film stars and singers, but the best picture of all is my best friend, Lucas. His cluttered, jet-black hair seemed more attractive than his charming, masculine looks. I miss him so much and his mischievous smile.

Oh no, it's happening, someone's broken into our hiding place, this is it, we're all going to die!

Goodbye Kitty, forever.

Kimberley Barrow (13)
Wallington High School For Girls, Surrey

UNTITLED

'I dare you,' Darrel whispered, 'I dare you to go to the old cottage and stay the night there - in Collin's room.'

I gulped. I had never been to the cottage before because all of the ghastly rumours that were sweeping round it. But I did it . . . I trudged up the path. I didn't know why I was here. The rumours were too scary, too believable. Especially the one about poor Collin whose sister, Charlotte and himself were murdered when they were living here fifty years ago, whose ghost now roams around the house searching for his sister's ghost who had disappeared.

I pushed open the door and stepped inside. A damp, musty smell approached me. I quickly walked up the stairs. I opened the door of one of the rooms and knew it was Collin's. Toys belonging to a young boy were neatly placed in corners. I huddled in a corner. I vowed not to fall asleep . . . just in case the rumours were true. Although suddenly my eyes felt so heavy and I felt so warm I drifted off into a deep sleep.

Suddenly I woke up. Everywhere around me was cold. I heard a voice. 'Michael.'
My name.
'Where's Charlotte?'
I got up. I looked around the room and screamed. Standing by the door was a pale outline of a boy.
'Michael, find my sister,' the ghost said, 'or the same thing that happened to me will happen to you.' He looked so fierce that I immediately believed him. I scrambled out of the door. I had no idea what his sister looked like or where she would be. For hours I searched the house. It was so creepy, looking at all the things that someone had used so many years ago. The kitchen was the worst room of all. It had large carving knives stuck on the wall and it smelt stale. I wondered if one of the knives had been what had been used to kill Charlotte. I shuddered at the thought and quickly went upstairs. I searched each room but I found nothing.

Suddenly I felt cold again. The hairs on the back of my neck stood on end. I swirled round. The boy was there. 'Have you found my sister?' he asked menacingly.

No, I'm s-sorry, I-I'm still looking,' I stammered.
'You had better find her,' he said, 'or else.'
I quickly turned away. I knew what 'or else' meant. I wasn't sure whether I believed what was happening. Maybe it was a cruel joke of Darrel's? I wasn't sure. I was about to go and find the boy so I could tell, but just as I was walking towards Collin's room I noticed a large door. I couldn't believe I hadn't noticed it before. I turned the knob. It surprisingly turned and the door opened quite easily. I sidled inside. I gasped at what I saw. It was a girl's room with dolls and soft animals everywhere. A small girl was sitting on the bed. She had a pale outline, just like the boy. I knew she was Charlotte. I noticed she was crying.
'I know where your brother is . . . he misses you,' I said, 'come with me and I'll take you to him.'
She got up and followed me back to Collin's room. I walked in, closely followed by Charlotte. He looked up and for the first time he actually smiled. He and Charlotte ran into each other's arms.
'Thank you,' Collin said to me before he and his sister ran off, hand in hand.

Bernice Tuckey (13)
Wallington High School For Girls, Surrey

LITTLE RED RIDING HOOD

Have you ever wondered what *really* happened in Little Red Riding Hood? Well, I am Wolf, the one that got axed, and I am going to tell you how it *really went.*

There was once a girl, aged seven, who people called Little Red Riding Hood. She was a malicious, vicious child who always wore red because it suited her personality. Her grandma, called Grandma, became ill and asked if someone *other than* Little Red could come and bring her some food. Little Red saw this as her opportunity to get all the money in Grandma's will, so with no hesitation ran through the woods with just a basket. Picture her running through the woods, throwing the boisterous bear, armed alligator, feline fox and other wildlife out of the way. She came to a complete halt to pick some fruits, which she thought were safe from a tree with an alarmed fence and a sign saying, *Beware Poisonous Fruit!*

She didn't realise I was watching her and got to Grandma's front door and burst in. Luckily I had got there first and switched places with Grandma who was hidden in the cupboard. I tried to scare her by showing her I was a wolf but she was a karate and origami expert, she threw me on the floor and went to get an axe man to attack me. Then freed Grandma and threw me out.

Now you have heard the *real* story just beware of Little Red Riding Hood.

Jessica Bembridge (13)
Wallington High School For Girls, Surrey

DAILY EXPRESS - BLOOD SOAKED BOY

World Exclusive

Cameron Kelsey, aged 14, of Larkin Road, Dealworth in London was drenched with blood by a woman.

Cameron Kelsey was coming out of the Leisure Centre with his friends, heading for a snack when he was faced by a woman with light, brown hair, smart charcoal grey suit. She also had a smiling face.

She looked very friendly and asked him 'Are you Cameron Kelsey, the pig-heart boy?'

Cameron nodded in reply.

The woman slowly brought out something from behind her back. It was a bucket, she held the bucket in one hand then with the other free hand to steady the bucket.

Cameron saw something red in it. He raised his hand to protect himself and in a matter of seconds he found himself drenched in blood and the woman was screaming at him 'Murderer! Murderer!'

Cameron was comforted by his best friend Marlon then by a group of people. The woman was still screaming at Cameron but the crowd stopped her from getting to him.

The police came after a while to the scene and asked Cameron a few questions and then took him to the hospital to recover from the coldness and stiffness he was suffering.

After a few minutes his mum and nan came to the hospital to comfort him, after the tragic moment that Cameron had come across and been the victim of.

Amina Zurgani (13)
Walthamstow School For Girls, London

SNOW WHITE

On a hot sunny day a girl called Snow White was working so hard that she thought she was going to faint, but she couldn't stop because the evil seven Dwarves would lock her up in a small, cramped bedroom without any food or water. She had no choice but to do all her chores as well as the other Dwarves' chores!

'What are you doing?' screamed Moany.

'Yeah! you were supposed to be cooking dinner, but you decided to stay in bed until four o'clock in the morning!' said Unhappy, in his deep Welsh voice.

'But I did get up early, unlike you and your other little friends, and you get the priviledge of staying asleep until eleven o'clock, so why can't I?' shouted Snow White very angrily.

'Well, because, because, err, hmmm - oh yes, because you're the maid and you have to get up early to cook our breakfasts and so on!' shouted Bossy.

'Get on with your work and don't ever speak to us like that again!' shouted all of the very, very angry Dwarves in their loudest voices. So Snow White carried on scrubbing the floor.

When she had finished, Snow White struggled to her feet and hobbled to the kitchen, rubbing her sore back, she ran some water, turned around and stared out of the window. She could see the huge castle which belonged to her Aunt - *The Queen* and thought, I could run away to my friendly Aunt, she will protect me.

So Snow White put the glass down, ran as fast as she could up the stairs to her tiny bedroom to pack her bags. Then when she got upstairs, Snow White opened her cupboard, grabbed a huge bag and threw it on her bed then rushed to her drawers. She threw all her clothes into the bag, with some shoes, flannels, towels and a brush. Snow White ran downstairs, bumping her bulging bag down the stairs after her. She did a packed lunch made up of chicken sandwiches, two bottles of water, a slice of home-made chocolate fudge, toffee and banana source. She packed it in her already bulging bag, put her coat over her shoulder and ran out of the door and up the hill.

Half an hour later she stood in front of her Aunt's castle and with all the strength she had left, she knocked on the door and waited a while, then a butler, tall and smart let her in with her Aunt waiting behind him to see who it was. As Snow White walked in, her Aunt jumped up and shouted in delight, *'Snow White!'*

'Aunt!' shouted Snow White.

'What are you doing here?' asked Snow White's Aunt, confused.

'Well I've run away from the Dwarves because they were really, really, really mean! And I thought of you and how kind you are and how you would let me stay with you. You do have room, don't you?' asked Snow White concerned.

'Of course, come and sit down and have a drink first, then you can tell me all about it!'

'Okay then,' said Snow White, pleased.

10 Minutes Later

'So they were that mean were they?' said Snow White's Aunt angrily.

'Yes!' answered Snow White.

'Okay, they are going to be banned from this land forever!'

And the next day the Dwarves were banned from the land.

Snow White was very pleased and didn't have to work again, after all her Aunt was the rich Queen! Then after two months, her Aunt died and Snow White became the new Queen and lived very happily ever after.

Emma Purdon (12)
Walthamstow School For Girls, London

WHAT A PARTY?

The party was a complete disaster. Well of course it started okay, but then the older kids came . . . let me start from the very beginning.

It was my twelfth birthday and I was having a disco. I invited nearly everyone whom I knew. We cleared out the living room for us to dance and we hired a DJ, we got loads of food and sweets and best of all Mum and Dad said that they would go out and come back at 12 o'clock.

Anyway as I said, it started off fine, everyone was dancing and eating. The DJ was playing our favourite songs and we were having loads of fun.

Suddenly at about 10 o'clock we heard loud shouting outside. We thought nothing of it and carried on dancing, but about five minutes later, the front door burst open and about 14 older boys and girls came rushing in!

I heard my friend Louise say, 'Oh no, they're gatecrashing the party!' They came in and started throwing food everywhere. They turned the music up, drunk loads of beer, started smoking and made a big mess! The worse thing was most of the people started to go home.

We were quite scared but the DJ phoned the police and the sirens scared them off. By this time there was only my friend and I left in the room. The house was such a mess! Mum and Dad came rushing in. It turned out that they were only next-door and when they heard the sirens they thought something was wrong.

We cleared up and the gatecrashers were told off by my dad the next day after school.

What a party!

Layla O'Driscoll-Kirkwood (13)
Walthamstow School For Girls, London

TICKING

We were nearly into the third lesson but still I was groggy and cross-eyed as though I'd just fallen out of bed. The teacher's voice boring into me like a long iron, being forced in by a big heavy metal hammer.

She sat down at her desk and eagerly began leafing through a magazine she'd confiscated from a girl earlier.

That was our cue, two people began twittering away (like the birds that wake you up in the mornings, during the spring), and gradually everyone joined in one by one.

I was okay for a while, then came the ticking (it was like rain dripping on to a hard metal surface) the colour drained from my face as the noise magnified 100 times louder (each tick was like the skin of a drum vibrating). Whilst this was going on I felt a big hot stone drop into my stomach, as it dropped I felt an explosion in my stomach, the heat was moving upwards, out of my stomach and into other parts of my body.

My temperature was rising and I could feel the sweat pouring out from my pores. My vision became unfocused and blurred, as I stared around in panic, I suddenly felt light-headed, my brain felt wrung out, it also felt as though someone was pinching and kneading it. Each pinch hit me right between the eyes, the pain was so intense I had to close my eyes.

Each breath was becoming harder to take in. In desperation I tried to stand up. There in mid-stand or mid-sit, everything was becoming dimmer, the noise of the class was fading. My hands and knees were shaking uncontrollably. I could feel myself buckle, and I did. I fell, fell into the deep darkness and reality of unconsciousness.

Sophia Choudhry (13)
Walthamstow School For Girls, London

CAMERON'S LETTER TO GRANNY

Dear Granny,

I am writing to tell you about my operation. As you know I haven't been very lucky with getting another human heart.

A doctor has offered me a heart transplant, but the heart is not coming from a human, it's coming from a pig. You may think it's against animal rights, but right now it's a situation of life and death and I would really like to have a normal life.

Sometimes I wish I'd never been born, because I feel like everything is my fault. Mum has dropped a big bombshell, that she's pregnant. Dad didn't even know!

I miss you very much, I wish you could be here because I feel very lonely and Mum and Dad keep arguing and I think it's because of me.

From your grandson
    Cameron

PS: Write back tell me what you think about the operation.
    See you soon.

Farah Targino (13)
Walthamstow School For Girls, London

TICKING

He stopped dead in his tracks. He couldn't let himself get caught this far ahead in the plan. He checked to his right, then to his left, not a soul in sight. It was his chance to make a break for it.

A trickle of cold sweat ran down his neck, his hands were clammy, he had never been so nervous before, but then again he had never been in charge of such a high profile project. He checked his ultra stylish, unknown to be a gadget, watch. Yep, it was time!

Tim Sullivan made a break for it. In this project, time meant everything, you had to be precise. You had to know when to move from one place to another, when and where precisely to dodge the lasers and most importantly of all, the final task.

Tim had managed to come face to face with the building itself, but he was having doubts. He didn't want to look like a coward, but he decided to chicken out. He just couldn't bring himself to do it and so he formulated a brilliant plan. That night when he fell asleep, he half felt a coward, but the other half felt like a scheming genius.

Hina Dadabhoy (13)
Walthamstow School For Girls, London

BOY'S POIGNANT LAST WORDS HIGHLIGHT CURRENT CRISIS

The family of Jake Clark, the 16-year-old who took his own life last month, after years of torment at the hands of bullies, yesterday released a poem which Jake, who had been described as 'exceptionally caring' and 'intelligent', wrote days before he took an overdose of sleeping tablets.

Olivia James, Jake's mother, told the children's charity, *SCEREF*, she hoped that by sharing with the public one of her son's last cries for help 'People will become aware of the increase in suicide attempts among young adults, and in particular men between the ages of 15 and 24. I believe that this issue must be highlighted and addressed by the community as a whole'.

The poem, entitled *Rites Of Passage,* is going to be incorporated into a new mental health initiative, designed to support young people and teachers in developing anti-bullying policies.

Rites Of Passage

Initiation.
An embrace,
A friendly gesture,
The Judas kiss.
Prince?

Disintegration.
A slap,
A poisoned apple.
Toad?

Banished from the realm,
Defences lulled.

Discarded,
New prey sought.

Stranded on the edge,
The dark isle,
Still mocked, taunted

Shy away from contact,
Crawl further into my shell.

A lone cry; pleading for support,
A lifeline,
Overlooked,
neglected, isolated.

Desperation descends,
Darkness falls,
Rapidly,
Seeping through the fragile shelter.
Will I drown?

On the horizon,
Advancing gradually,
The warm glow of true friendship,
Will it arrive?
Can it free me?
Unlock the shackles?
A rite of passage?

Niamh Collard (13)
Walthamstow School For Girls, London

A DAY IN THE LIFE OF GREGORY THE CAT

You know, I'm getting sick and tired of the name Tiddles. I mean what a soppy name. Tiddles, I ask you? Out of all the perfectly good cat names in the back garden, Emily had to choose Tiddles. Now all the cats who come to do their 'business' in my back garden, tease me. But they all know I'm really called Gregory, so they insist on shouting from the lilac tree at the bottom of the garden 'Oh Tiddles, Mummy wants you!' That really annoys me!

Anyway, I've now spent three days in this house with Emily and her family, and already I'm not allowed in the sitting room.

Yesterday, whilst the family were in the kitchen. I snuck in and there was a large tank full of water in the corner of the room, there were some strange life-forms moving around in it. They were brightly coloured and very rude! I went up to the tank and tapped on the glass with my paw; and the creatures just kept moving. Wait a minute, I've just been told that they were 'swimming'. Thank you Cheers!

So back to the story. There I am looking at swimming creatures, but they were annoying me so much that I had to jump up on the rim of the tank. It was very thin. The creatures were still swimming around. I began to think about swimming all day and all night. I was so wrapped up in thought, that I fell in. Damn it was cold! I was later rescued by Emily's father, who didn't look too happy!

So that's the end of my first ever diary entry in the Emily household. I'll write tomorrow.

This is Gregory the cat, signing off.

Miriam Billing (13)
Walthamstow School For Girls, London

Two In One Of A Name

One night just after five o'clock at the YMCA where my mum works.

There was a woman called Georgina, she stayed behind for a bit longer than usual and she was just sitting there when a woman (the cleaner) said, 'Hi, what's your name? Staying on a bit later tonight?'
'My name's George, I've got a lot of work to do.'

Five minutes later George (short for Georgina) got up and went to another department. Two minutes later the cleaner comes to the same department as George.
'Hello, what's your name? I've just seen someone who looks just like you.'
'That must have been my sister George, anyway my name is Gina,' said George.

The cleaner still thinks that George and Gina are sisters, but it's really just *Georgina!*

Emma Stonestreet (13)
Walthamstow School For Girls, London